The Last Book Party

Praise for *The Last Book Party*

"I tore through this novel in a single night. Intensely charming, intelligent, sexy, and specific, *The Last Book Party* immerses us in the incestuous world of the 1980s literary elite, from boozy, publicist-thrown parties in Manhattan to the writing nooks of a *New Yorker* staff writer on Cape Cod. The novel's narrator, Eve, has all the insecurities and doubts of any twenty-five-year-old aspiring writer but doesn't let those stop her from being a compelling, bold, active heroine in charge of her own life. This is the summer's most delicious and intelligent beach read."

—Julia Phillips, author of *Disappearing Earth*
(finalist for National Book Award)

"*The Last Book Party* is a delight. Reading this story of a young woman trying to find herself while surrounded by the bohemian literary scene during a summer on the Cape in the late '80s, I found myself nodding along in so many moments and dreading the last page. Karen Dukess has rendered a wonderful world to spend time in."

—Taylor Jenkins Reid, *New York Times*
bestselling author of *Daisy Jones & The Six*

"A funny, sweetly melancholy novel about youth, age, romance, the seashore, and, always, books—writing them, reading them, and learning all they can and cannot teach us. What a pleasure to attend Karen Dukess's *The Last Book Party*."

—Cathleen Schine, *New York Times* bestselling author of
The Three Weissmanns of Westport and *The Grammarians*

"Karen Dukess plants a bright flag on the dunes with her debut. . . . Dukess delivers a spare, bittersweet page-turner. . . . [Her] unmistakable love of words, stories, and 'book people' is what keeps you bobbing briskly along with the waves."

—Elisabeth Egan, *The New York Times Book Review*

"*The Last Book Party* is at once delightfully gossipy and intellectually serious, an ode to literature and a warning against hero-worship."

—Lily Meyer, *Electric Literature*

"This coming-of-age novel offers up a healthy dose of late '80s nostalgia, and it's a breezy read for book enthusiasts."

—*O, The Oprah Magazine*

"Part coming of age, part gossipy peek into the enclave of writers, editors, poets, and artists who annually escaped the heat of Boston and New York to talk, drink, and work on Cape Cod, this semi-nostalgic debut is the ideal summer read for book people."

—*Library Journal* (starred review)

"Readers aching for the sun-dappled intrigue of André Aciman's *Call Me by Your Name* or the wit of Francine Prose's *Blue Angel* will find a kindred reading experience here. . . . Mixing ambivalence, nostalgia, and the power of innocence in an idyllic setting, this journey of self-discovery is an ideal summer read for those who might shun more typical 'beach-read' offerings."

—*Booklist*

"This beautiful novel manages to be both a delightful page-turner and a luminous coming-of-age story that grapples with themes of ambition, family, love, and how it feels to be a young woman finding her way in the world for the first time. I loved it."

—Whitney Scharer, author of *The Age of Light*

"*The Last Book Party* captures a world tantalizingly close to the surface of memory, in which things now lost to time mattered a great deal, and the Internet era was slouching toward us to be born. This orphic book goes down to retrieve a beloved New York, and the pleasant ache at its heart is that it can't bring [the city] back forever. Charming, lovely, and written with a light touch, this book captures the longing and unease of summer romance amid the complexity of postgraduate life. Shades of [Philip Roth's] *Goodbye, Columbus*, [Michael Chabon's] *The Mysteries of Pittsburgh*, and [Jay McInerney's] *Bright Lights, Big City* haunt its pages."

—Matthew Thomas, *New York Times* bestselling author of *We Are Not Ourselves*

The *Last*
Book Party

a novel

KAREN DUKESS

A Holt Paperback

Henry Holt and Company   New York

Holt Paperbacks
Henry Holt and Company
Publishers since 1866
120 Broadway
New York, New York 10271
www.henryholt.com

A Holt Paperback® and ® are registered
trademarks of Macmillan Publishing Group, LLC.

The Library of Congress has cataloged the hardcover edition as follows:

Names: Dukess, Karen, author.
Title: The last book party : a novel / Karen Dukess.
Description: First edition. | New York : Henry Holt and Company, 2019.
Identifiers: LCCN 2018046715 | ISBN 9781250225474 (hardcover)
Classification: LCC PS3604.U446 L37 2019 | DDC 813/.6—dc23
LC record available at https://lccn.loc.gov/2018046715

ISBN 9781250774422 (trade paperback)

Our books may be purchased in bulk for promotional, educational,
or business use. Please contact your local bookseller or the Macmillan
Corporate and Premium Sales Department at (800) 221-7945, extension
5442, or by e-mail at MacmillanSpecialMarkets@macmillan.com.

Originally published in hardcover in 2019 by Henry Holt and Company

First Holt Paperbacks Edition 2020

Designed by Kelly S. Too

Printed in the United States of America

1 3 5 7 9 10 8 6 4 2

For Steve, Joe, and Johnny

"But how could you live and have no story to tell?"

Fyodor Dostoyevsky, *White Nights*

part one

June 1987

1

Walking up the dirt driveway to the summer home of Henry Grey, I reminded myself that I was an invited guest. Men in wrinkled linen shirts and baggy pants and women in loose, flowing skirts and dresses milled about on the ragged lawn in front of the old saltbox house. The wind off the ocean, a few hollows away, was gentle but steady, sending cocktail napkins floating like feathers.

Looking down at my flat espadrilles and wishing I had worn heels, I heard a woman say, "His ego's as big as his canvas." And from beyond her, a man's booming voice: "What I should have said was 'Edna St. Vincent Millay.' What I said? 'Edna St. Vincent Mulcahy!'" The speaker and his listeners roared with laughter. I took a few steps toward the crowd. A patrician man with a shock of white hair jostled his drink and said to his companion, "I knew Bob Gottlieb would usher in change, but I had hoped it would be more substantial than allowing the word *fucking* in *The New Yorker*."

The guests were acting just as I had imagined they would. This was Truro's summer elite, the writers, editors, poets, and artists who left their apartments in Manhattan and Boston around

Memorial Day and stayed on Cape Cod into September. I knew of this circle from the occasional Talk of the Town piece and the gossip of my parents and their friends, who relished sharing a summer town with such famous intellectuals, even if they rarely crossed paths.

This crowd spent the summer in weathered, shingled Cape houses with screened porches, not tidy, new summer homes with open decks like the one my parents had purchased after years of renting. They played backgammon, drank gin, and gathered for endless round-robin tennis tournaments, not at Olivers' in Wellfleet, where my parents and their friends paid by the hour, but on their own scruffy courts. With a few exceptions, they weren't Jewish like us. As far as I knew, they didn't even go to the beach.

I made my way through a group of people surrounding a wooden table, disappointed to discover it held nothing but a platter of deviled eggs and a small bowl of mixed nuts. Did the scant amount of food explain why everyone seemed so thin, their bodies as straight as their hair? I didn't consider myself over-weight, just a little soft around the edges, but as I stood among these angular people in my floral Laura Ashley sundress with its fitted bodice, I felt shamefully curvy.

Self-conscious about standing alone, I approached an old farmhouse table where two men were shucking oysters in a way that suggested a friendly competition. They were both tanned and solid, but one was young, maybe just a few years older than I was, with shiny brown hair pulled into a ponytail; the other was older, with wavy dark hair. When the older man looked up, I saw it was Henry Grey. He looked kinder and more handsome than the forbidding photograph on the jacket of his collection of columns, *My New Yorker*.

I introduced myself to Henry. He blinked.

"From Hodder, Strike and Perch?" I said. "Malcolm Wing's secretary?"

Henry put down his shucking knife and threw his hands up in the air. "My God, Eve Rosen, you exist! The only actual human being employed by Hodder, Strike!"

Henry's boisterous welcome set me at ease. The younger oyster shucker reached out his hand, still in a thick canvas glove.

"Happy to know you exist," he said, with an easy, open smile. "I'm Franny, Henry's indentured servant and son."

I took his damp glove. Bits of oyster shell dug into my fingers as he clasped my hand. His eyes were an arresting green.

"Happy to know you exist too," I said.

The sun had begun to slide down in the sky and was casting a honeyed light on everything. The tips of the long, wispy grass behind Franny appeared lit up.

It had never occurred to me that Henry might have a son, as our correspondence had been strictly business. His letters, which arrived by mail even when Henry was home in Manhattan, were composed on a manual typewriter, on crisp little pieces of ecru stationery with the initials *HCG* engraved in black ink. He wrote only a few lines, usually about something mundane like missing royalty statements, but always with great wit and biting sarcasm about Malcolm's lack of attention. It was exciting to exchange letters with a *New Yorker* writer, even one who received so little respect around our office, due in part to his endless memoirs, which had been contracted by an editor who had retired long ago and were yet to be published. I spent considerable time crafting notes back to Henry, trying to be helpful while also sounding effortlessly funny and smart. Our correspondence was the highlight of my job.

Henry held out an oyster. "For you, the sole employee of Hodder, Strike and Perch deserving of a mollusk so fresh."

I took the oyster and brought the shell to my mouth, conscious of both Franny and Henry watching as I slurped it down as delicately as I could manage.

"Briny and sweet?" Henry asked.

I nodded and wiped my mouth. I was struck by the men's resemblance.

"Looking at the two of you is like flipping from Henry Past to Franny Future. You must get that all the time."

"And looking at you is like downing a shot from the fountain of youth," Henry said. "Another oyster?"

"OK, Henry, simmer down," Franny said.

"Do you always call him Henry?" I asked, taking the second oyster.

"When it's called for."

Henry pushed his knife into the seam of a fresh oyster and opened it easily. He tossed the empty half in a bucket and, holding the filled shell in a gloved hand, flicked a few flakes from the flesh inside before setting it on a platter of ice at the end of the table. Looking at me, he spoke to Franny. "My boy, this young lady is a marvel of efficiency. And not at all what I expected. When I learned of her connection to Truro and invited her to join us, I was prepared to meet a skinny spinster in a cardigan sweater."

Franny looked my way, shaking his head, and pointed his shucking knife toward his father. "He is such a relic."

I stepped to the side of the table so other guests could get oysters but stayed close enough to continue the conversation. Bantering with Henry in person was more challenging than on paper, but I was determined to keep up. And it was easier than talking to Franny, whose good looks unnerved me.

"Is efficiency generally unattractive?" I asked Henry.

Still grinning, he nodded. "I have found it to be so."

Franny took off his shucking gloves and tossed them on the table.

"OK, it's time for a break," he said, with a dazzling smile. "C'mon, Eve, I'll show you around."

Henry looked at Franny and then back at me. "Yes, of course, by all means, join our young brethren. But, Eve, really—if you ever need a job, I'm on the lookout for an efficient research assistant for the summer."

I laughed. He couldn't be serious. "It would be a tough commute from New York, but I'll keep it in mind."

I followed Franny up the hill toward the house. Looking back, I saw Henry watching us. I gave a little wave. Henry tapped his oyster knife to his forehead in a quick salute.

Franny stopped outside the screened porch. "So are you a writer too?" he asked. He pulled the rubber band from his hair, which swung down and brushed his broad shoulders.

"I'd like to be. But it's hard until you know what you want to say."

"Is it?" he said.

"I suppose it's easy for you, growing up with it and everything."

"Nope. Books are not my thing."

He stated it as a simple fact, one which I found hard to believe, considering who his parents were. I was sure that if my parents were writers, rather than a tax attorney and a part-time interior decorator, I'd be further along toward becoming one myself.

Franny cocked his head. I heard the jumpy beat of "Walk Like an Egyptian."

"I think there's dancing," Franny said.

He led me through the porch and inside, where the furniture had been pushed back to the walls and the rugs rolled up. A younger crowd was dancing barefoot in the living room and dining room. The kitchen was filled with people standing in small groups or sitting on counters, drinking beer and talking. Everyone seemed happy to see Franny, grabbing his hand or tousling his hair or swallowing him in a hug. A little girl scampered up and wrapped her arms around his waist, squeezing until he swept her up onto his shoulders and danced around the kitchen. When he set her down, she skipped away, and he turned to a short, wrinkled old woman with her gray hair knotted in a bun on the top of her head. She had paint on her hands and Birkenstocks peeking out from beneath a long black skirt. Franny rested his hands on her shoulders and, leaning in and talking loudly so she could hear him over the music, promised to come soon to photograph her work.

Franny introduced me to some friends and cousins as "a writer friend of Henry's from New York," which everyone accepted so readily that I gave up trying to explain over the music that I was a mere editorial secretary. As much as I wanted to be a writer, my habit of starting stories and ripping them up after a few pages didn't give me the right to call myself one.

"This is Rosie Atkinson—video artist," Franny said, kissing the cheek of a petite young woman with a jet-black bob and magenta lips. "How goes the installation?" Before she could answer, a cherubic guy wearing round glasses and a faded Brooks Brothers shirt grabbed Franny from behind, bellowing, "Franster!"

Franny whipped around.

"My man!" They hugged again. "Eve, remember this name— Stephen Frick. This goofy-looking creature is on a fast track to becoming a famous composer."

Creativity was clearly this crowd's currency. Franny's introductions each included some artistic cachet: Up-and-coming playwright. Jazz saxophonist. Gallery manager. Actor. There didn't seem to be a preprofessional among them—none of the law school or med school students, junior consultants, or account executives found among the children of my parents' friends. From years of vacationing in Truro, I'd been vaguely aware of this crowd, but never expected to be hanging out with them, let alone being welcomed as if I belonged.

The party had an easy, unscripted feel. Two barefoot boys in overalls ran through the kitchen, one with a bag of marshmallows. Three women sat on the steep wooden steps of the back staircase engaged in what seemed to be serious conversation. I grabbed a Corona from an old washtub on the counter and took a few quick gulps. Someone turned up the music, and Franny started dancing as he gently pushed me and several of the people in the kitchen into the dining room. At first, I danced awkwardly, wishing I hadn't worn a prissy cotton dress. But as I finished that first beer, I began to relax. I kicked my sandals into the corner and twirled into the center of the room, where I was happy to catch Franny's eyes a few times and be spun by him, though I wasn't sure if he was dancing with me or with everyone. As it grew darker, more people came inside until the house was packed.

In the living room, Henry danced with a slim, long-necked woman in a floor-length halter dress patterned with swirls of orange and green, her graying hair swinging in a thick braid down her back. I assumed she was his wife, Tillie Sanderson, whose poems I had tried to understand when I was at Brown. Henry and Tillie and the rest of the older set looked loose and happy in a way that made them seem not only younger than my own parents, though they were ostensibly the same age, but ageless, as if being artists and writers freed them from anything as conventional as growing old. Henry and Tillie, laughing, looked like they were doing "the bump." I tried to imagine my parents dancing to the Talking Heads or doing the bump, but it was impossible. Just then Franny appeared and grabbed my hands.

"What's so funny?" he asked, spinning me beneath his arms.

"This," I said. It was clear he had no idea what I was talking about.

Once every summer, my parents had a party too. Instead of barefoot dancing, rolled-up rugs, and old women in Birkenstocks, a cocktail party hosted by my parents demanded a strict headcount, from which would be calculated the number of mini quiches required to guarantee four per person; tailored summer outfits purchased at Filene's in the Chestnut Hill mall; and, in every bathroom, freshly ironed embroidered hand towels and trays of soaps shaped like scallop shells.

I had been vacationing in Truro since I was a child, and each summer was as predictable as the tides. On sunny days, we would go to Ballston Beach, where we would spread our blankets to the right of the entrance, never the left. If the ocean was stinky with mung, we would go to Corn Hill to swim in the bay, where, when the wind died, it was easy to skip a flat rock six times over the water's glassy surface. My parents would unfold beach chairs and read: my mother multigenerational, from-the-shtetl-to-Scarsdale family sagas, my father the latest Book of the Month Club presidential biography or the stock tables. My brother, Danny, and I would dive for fiddler crabs or swim. The pattern adjusted, without really changing, as we got older. Instead of frolicking in the water, I would lose myself in novels while Danny tackled the problems in the Mathematical Games columns in *Scientific American*.

On the last night of our vacation, we would buy lobsters and boil them in a big black pot. When we returned home to

Newton, we'd shake the sand from our beach clothes and, like someone had flicked a switch, restart our old routine: work, school, dinner at six, my parents' praise for Danny's genius at math, and their gentle annoyance with my dreamy bookishness. This mold, set so long ago, endured.

Even now, my parents obsessed about Danny's trajectory through grad school at MIT, their hopes for familial greatness fully staked on him, while they waited for me to abandon my dream of becoming a writer and buckle down to go to law school or get a teaching degree. Lately, I also had been doubting my path, wondering how I could be serious about an ambition that had yet to yield results more notable than the piles of paper scattered about my room.

But watching Franny dance, his long hair flipping around him, I was buoyed by a sense of possibility. A tentative belief that I could have a creative life too. It was intoxicating to have spun my way into Franny's orbit and this other Truro. And now that I had, I didn't want to let it go.

2

Late the next morning, I awoke to the drippings of a rain that had passed through while I slept. A thick fog hung in the air, hiding the marsh and the harbor beyond. The way it surrounded the house, blurring the view outside, added to my sense that the night before had been a dream, leaving me with vivid yet unconnected images: being swept into an improvised tango by an old man who looked like Albert Einstein; crowding onto the screened porch when Henry recited a creepy yet mesmerizing old poem, "The Cremation of Sam McGee"; wandering the second floor in search of a bathroom and coming upon Henry and Tillie's bedroom, which was adorned with so many half-burned candles that it looked like a shrine.

On the way downstairs to our kitchen, I heard my mother on the phone.

"Yes, the Head of the Summer party. Yes, *head*—like *Head Of The Charles,* I think. I suppose it's their idea of humor. No, I didn't get details. She came in very late."

My mother would want to hear about the party but would probably feign only mild interest. She hadn't hidden her surprise that I'd been invited—in fact, she'd made it clear that she thought Henry had extended the invitation without the expectation I would go. Her reaction was in keeping with her odd fascination—she was both enamored and scornful—with Henry and Tillie's crowd.

When I'd begun working at Hodder, Strike, she'd seemed impressed by my connection to Henry. But she never failed to tell me when she'd read something about *The New Yorker* having passed its prime. She sent me articles about the recent ousting of legendary editor William Shawn, circling with a red pen where Henry was cited as an example of how stale and indulgent much of the magazine's writing had become. Just recently, she'd told me with barely disguised glee that Henry's three-part series on the interstate highway system had been brutally ridiculed in *Spy* magazine.

"They said that he's never met a fact he didn't fall in love with, that he's *infactuated*," she'd said.

"Since when do suburban interior decorators read *Spy?*" I'd asked.

She'd frowned at my jab. "I like to stay current." And then, "A client of mine gave it to me. Her son-in-law sells ad space in *Spy*."

When I walked into the kitchen, my mother was off the phone. On the table was a basket of blueberry muffins.

"Nice time last night?" she asked, putting plates in the dishwasher.

"Very." I poured a cup of coffee and went outside onto the deck to avoid her questions. I would give her some details later, but for now I wanted to savor the sense of being at the party. It was a rare experience for me to want to stay at a party rather than leave early to go home and read.

The fog was lifting slowly, revealing the hills of wild grass

and bearberry that rolled down to the marsh, where soon enough
I could see grayish pools of water and feathery islands of grass.
As I sipped my coffee, the houses on the other side of the marsh
came into view, emerging from the mist like images sharpening on
a Polaroid. I loved how kindly the weather changed on mornings
like this, as if sparing you the shock of awakening into a bright,
clear day and instead taking your hand and gently guiding you
from the cloud of sleep.

A car pulled into the gravel driveway; my mother's ride had
arrived, and she'd be leaving for her aerobics class in Wellfleet,
which meant I could go inside for breakfast without being interrogated. When I heard the front door close, I went into the kitchen.

As I peeled the paper from a muffin, my mother poked her
head back inside. She looked as orderly as ever, a pink terry
headband keeping her dark hair in place. "Dad's out fishing. Be
a love and pick up some skim milk and a bottle of olive oil. You
can check out Jams; it's quite nice."

I was surprised to hear a good word about Jams, which had
been disparaged by several people at the party for its high prices
and unfortunate catering to the growing contingent of "yuppie"
families summering in Truro. There was a lot of nostalgia in town
for Schoonejongen's, the dusty old general store that Jams had
replaced, and widespread disappointment, which I shared, that
the battered old post office on the hill, with its FBI Most Wanted
posters by the door, had been closed and relocated to a bland
box of a building next to Jams. These changes were not seen as
improvements, at least by summer people, though complaining
about Schooney's, as the old store was known, had been a Truro
ritual for decades.

It had been impossible to shop at Schooney's without being
barked at by Ellie Schoonejongen, a doughy woman with thin-
ning, white-blond hair who spent her days slumped by the cash

register complaining that customers bought either too much or too little. Once, when my mother and I stopped by to get fruit for the beach, Ellie shrieked, "Only three peaches? Take four!" When my mother took another peach to appease her, Ellie sneered and said under her breath that there was no price too high for summer people to pay. Truro's seasonal crowd embraced the unpretentiousness of Schooney's, as they did the irony of the TRURO CENTER sign on Route 6, which marked the tiny settlement of a handful of buildings—the slightly rundown shingled building that was now home to Jams, the institutional-looking post office, a small Realtor's office that handled summer rentals, and an unassuming news shop called Dorothy's, whose most important purpose was ensuring that every summer visitor who so desired could get a copy of the Sunday *New York Times*.

What drew people to Truro was its unspoiled and open beauty. Just south of Provincetown, with its gay bars, restaurants, and art galleries, Truro was Cape Cod's most rural town, with well over half of it containing the vast protected forests, sand dunes, and empty ocean beaches of the Cape Cod National Seashore. The rest of the town, which stretched only a few miles from the ocean to the calmer waters of the Cape Cod Bay, was marsh and rolling hills and winding roads, some paved and some little more than rutted dirt paths, along which were simple saltbox houses and newer summer homes.

When I opened the screen door to Jams, I caught a whiff of the sweet smell of fresh-baked pastries. The store was bright and clean, with buttery, wide-plank wooden floors. Along with staple groceries, the shelves now held luxuries like Camembert and Brie, marinated artichokes, and imported olives. A deli had been added in back, which offered rotisserie chickens, baguettes, and a menu of sandwiches named for Truro beaches: the Corn Hill, for the spot where, as every Truro resident knew,

Myles Standish and his band of Pilgrims landed before heading to Plymouth, was turkey with coleslaw. Watching fit women with bright rattan beach bags order cold Chicken Marbella and pasta salad with pesto, I understood why my mother liked Jams and why the night before Henry had pronounced that he would never step foot in the place.

After locating milk and olive oil, I circled the store again, hoping I might run into Franny, which I knew was as unlikely as my standing a chance with him. He was clearly something of a ladies' man, but I couldn't help wanting to see him again. It wasn't just his beautiful eyes and smile or the casual way he had grabbed me to dance. It was also his warmth and instant acceptance of me into the fold that had made me feel aglow, as if I had not only belonged at the party, but might become the writer he'd thought I already was. I wanted to be back in that house, but with all the guests gone. Brimming with books and magazines, paintings and photographs, the house was filled with items chosen because they were beloved and had a cherished story to tell, not because they matched the rest of the décor.

Before heading back home, I pulled over at the Cobb Memorial Library, just up the road from Truro Center. Alva Snow, the town's longtime librarian, was one of my favorite people in Truro. Alva, who looked much younger than her seventy-two years, had lived in Truro her whole life. She knew everything about everyone, not just the permanent residents but also the summer people, whom she called "wash ashores." For most of my childhood, I had regarded Alva much as I had the one-room library's old furniture, which was worn, comfortable, and not particularly memorable. But the summer before I left for college, after she noted that I was one of the few people who visited the library on sunny days as well as on rainy days, Alva and I began to have longer conversations, which were always rambling and fun. We talked about books, of course, which may be why I felt more comfortable with Alva than with most of the high school girls I knew, who were more interested in discussing television shows like *Dallas*. Alva loved the detective novels of Ngaio Marsh and P. D. James and nineteenth-century French poetry, while I liked getting lost in long novels of varying literary repute, everything from *The Thorn Birds* to *My Ántonia*. For a librarian, not to mention one getting on in years, Alva could be surprisingly girlish and silly. The summer after my freshman year, we talked about how much we wanted to believe the apocryphal story that the mayor of Providence, Buddy Cianci, planned to marry someone named Nancy Ann, so that she could be introduced in the Rhode Island Statehouse as "the esteemed Nancy Ann Cianci." Every time we said this, we collapsed in laughter, with Alva once giggling so much she began to hiccup uncontrollably.

When I walked into the musty library, Alva was at her desk gently trying to pry apart two pages of a picture book.

"Should I come back later—or will the impending diatribe against the evils of chewing gum be brief?"

Alva put down the book and smiled.

"I was wondering when you would show up. Please tell me you have finally arranged to spend an entire summer here."

"Nope, just a long weekend," I said, sitting in the wooden rocking chair beside her desk. "I came up for a party at Henry Grey's. First time I ever met him. Tell me: How did I not know he had a son?"

Alva took off her glasses and let them hang from the chain around her neck. She folded her hands on the desk and leaned toward me.

"The plot thickens," she said.

"What do you know about him?"

"He was a delightful child, as I recall. He was not much of a reader, however, but was quite the artist. He had his first exhibit of photographs in this very room when he was fifteen. Portraits of fishermen that he printed himself. Not a bad eye."

"Not bad to look at either," I said.

"You know what they say about judging a book by its cover," Alva said, with a sly smile.

"Because you're a librarian, I'll let you get away with that."

Remembering the milk in my car, I told Alva I had to leave to get my groceries home. In response, she took an old hardcover from a stack of books on her desk, opened the back cover, and stamped the "due by" card on the last page. It was one of my favorites, *I Capture the Castle* by Dodie Smith.

"How do you always do that?" I asked, flipping through the pages. "I read this years ago and absolutely loved it."

I stretched out my hand to return the book, but she didn't take it. She put her glasses back on and peered over them at me, saying, "Well, then, you'll enjoy reading it again."

3

After a late lunch, with Franny still on my mind, I decided to bike to the beach. I changed into my favorite T-shirt and shorts, then pulled my thick hair back and clipped it loosely with a barrette, letting a few strands hang down by my face. I smudged on some brown eyeliner, pleased that it made me appear a little older without looking like I was wearing makeup.

I set out toward the ocean and flew fast down Castle Road and along the marsh toward Truro Center. After riding beneath Route 6, I turned onto North Pamet Road, a longer route to the ocean, but one that would take me by Franny's. The air was surprisingly cool, suggesting that the ocean was still fogged in. Paying little attention to the turns in the road, I tried to figure out what I would say if I got up the nerve to stop in. As I approached the house, I slowed down to look through the beach plum bushes toward the tennis court. I heard the pop of tennis balls being hit and then a woman's shout, "Gin for the win!" I got off my bike and was walking along the edge of the road, peering through the thicket to see who was on the court, when a branch snapped beside me. I turned to find Franny.

"What do you think? Are they cheating?" he asked, pointing a pair of hedge clippers toward the court.

"Oh my God, you scared me." Embarrassed at being caught snooping, I tried desperately to think of an amusing excuse to explain myself. "Yes, there were reports of cheating, which was why the tennis police sent me."

"The tennis police?" Franny looked amused. I wished I had come up with something wittier. "Trust me. That tennis game is not even worth watching. By this time of day, they're generally too tipsy to keep score, let alone play well. And after last night, everyone's a little shaky."

"It was pretty wild," I said, remembering how I'd danced at the party. When my white-haired tango partner had dipped me back so low that my head was nearly touching the floor, I'd seen Franny watching from the corner of the dining room.

Franny looked up at the white expanse of sky.

"Not much of a beach day," he said.

"I like the ocean on days like this."

"Me too. Want company?"

He suggested I leave my bike on the side of the driveway so we could walk down together. After a few minutes of silence, I asked Franny how he had decided to become an artist. He seemed surprised by the question.

"It's just what I always did, who I am," he said. He'd gone to art school in Chicago, which he hated because it was "all theory and no fun."

"Really? That's what it was like in some of my literature classes," I said. "It was text, subtext, and literary theory, like we were dissecting frogs instead of reading books."

"All head and no heart?"

"Exactly," I said. "It made me even more self-conscious and critical of my own writing than I was before."

"That's why I dropped out of art school," Franny said.

"You just up and left?"

"Yup. An easy and excellent decision."

It had never occurred to me that the problem might be Brown and not me.

Franny had spent the past several years in New Orleans and Santa Fe, working in restaurants and bars so he'd have time to paint and take photographs. He was back east for the summer to figure out where to go next. "Possibly Maine," he said, as we walked past the path to the old cranberry bog and up toward the youth hostel. We could see the back side of the dunes by the ocean, the windswept landscape beautifully empty of people.

At the top of the bluff, Franny stopped in front of the hostel, an imposing white building that was once a Coast Guard station. He told me about his dream to paint a mural on the entire ocean-facing side of the building. "I see it as larger-than-life fishermen, maybe whalers, in bold strokes and dark, stormy colors." The way he spoke, his idea didn't sound like a vague artistic fantasy, but a pronouncement that the old building would be his canvas, that if he wanted to make it happen, it would.

Franny was completely comfortable with his identity as an artist in a way that astounded me. I thought of all the stories I had started and thrown away, rarely thinking one was good enough. When I did finish, I kept the stories to myself, shying from criticism and the risk of exposing a side of myself—angry, biting, needy—that I had learned to keep hidden.

"How can this place not inspire you?" Franny said. "You could write a thousand stories of things that might happen here."

As we descended toward the parking lot, I told him about a

story I'd written in middle school about a girl walking along the towering sand dunes at Longnook Beach who falls into a secret dwelling created inside the dune by a mysterious boy.

"She marvels at his hideaway, which has a table and a chair, if you can believe it, and he tells her how he created it, somehow defying physics and propping up the mountain of sand with planks of wood. They talk for a long time, until they hear a rumbling that gets louder and louder."

"What was it?" he asked.

"It was . . . the Wave."

Franny raised his eyebrows, waiting for more.

"That's it. That was the last line of the story. They were washed away. Awful, I know," I said. "The story won a prize, and I had to read it to the entire seventh grade. Kids made fun of me for weeks, coming up to me in the cafeteria and whispering, 'It was . . . *the Wave*.'" Daunted by the attention and the ridicule, I didn't write another story for several years.

Franny laughed. "It sounds like a great story."

The parking lot was empty. The air was misty, and the ocean's steady roar got louder as we walked up the path between the low dunes, reminding me how unpredictable and inconsistent the Cape weather was, that it could be clear at the bay and blustery here. We had the beach to ourselves. The wind was stiff, and the surf was still churned up from a recent storm. Waves crashed in every direction, ruffling the shore. We left our shoes by the entrance path and walked to the water. A buoy from a lobster pot was bobbing in the foam. It was unusual to see one so close to shore; it must have been pulled in by the storm. Franny looked at the buoy, then at me, and, with a whoop, ran into the water. I stood on the wet sand and watched as he jumped around like a little kid. Every time he got close to the buoy, the ocean sucked it under, and he would spin around, bewildered.

"There!" I yelled, as it popped up again. "There!"

He leapt at it again and again, waving for me to join him. "Come on!" he called.

I'd been warned more times than I could remember about the dangers of a riptide, even in shallow water. But Franny was having so much fun. Before I could change my mind, I ran and leapt into the foamy water and waded through the surf until I was beside him as he continued trying to grab the buoy. Chasing it, we bumped into each other and fell into the surf. Franny grinned and slapped his hand down on the water, sending a big splash up onto my face and shoulders. I shrieked and scooped water toward him, throwing it at his already-drenched T-shirt. He seemed not at all surprised that I was there, as if this were the kind of impulsive thing I did all the time.

Finally, the buoy surfaced in front of Franny.

"Grab it!" I yelled.

He lunged, fell onto his knees in the surf, and then came up, holding the rope. I jumped through the waves and grabbed the rope, which was slick with seaweed. We held on, bracing our legs in the sand and trying not to fall forward as the waves receded. The pull of the water was strong and the lobster trap was heavy. But when the water rushed in, we were able to run toward the beach and drag the trap behind us. We were pulled in, and pushed back, and in again, and out again until finally an enormous wave rolled in, and we managed to run and pull in enough rope to drag the lobster pot into shallow water and then carry it onto dry sand.

We threw ourselves down beside the wooden trap and looked at each other, soaked and triumphant, catching our breath. I turned around to see an old couple up on top of the dune waving at us. They were yelling something, their words lost in the wind and the crashing of the surf.

Franny threw his head back and hollered, "That was incredible!"

He was panting and smiling like a child. I was brimming with energy and excitement, feeling as unlatched as I had dancing in the dining room the night before. "Incredible!" I agreed. I whipped my head back and forth like a dog to get the water out of my hair. Franny laughed. And then we turned our attention to the lobster trap. Inside were two dark brownish lobsters.

Franny unhooked the pot and grabbed the lobsters by the tails and tossed them onto the sand. I glanced back toward the couple, worried they would warn us against taking the lobsters, but their hands were raised over their heads. They were applauding.

"Are you sure we should?" I asked.

"It's fine," Franny said, looking at the lobsters with pride. "It's not like we swam out and pulled the pot from the ocean. It practically washed up at our feet."

Franny took the lobsters and, facing the water, stretched his arms up into the air above his head, the lobsters nearly touching each other. The wind lifted his hair in a swirl. He dropped his arms and turned toward me with a mischievous grin.

"Boiled or baked?"

We started back to the house, each of us holding a lobster by the tail in one hand and our shoes in the other, comfortably silent on either side of the line in the road.

4

The inside of the house was dark and worn, like an old ship. A candle burned on a table in the kitchen, its wax dripping into little mountains on a faded cotton tablecloth. We put the lobsters in the sink. Franny gave me a pair of sweatpants and an old wool sweater to change into and directed me to the hall bathroom, where I was amused to find a stack of old *New Yorkers* in a basket by the toilet. The sweater, which smelled like whiskey, was big and soft, the V of its neck dipping almost too low. In the mirror, I was pleased to see that the wind and the water had left me with pink cheeks. I unclipped my barrette and let my hair hang down in unruly waves.

In the kitchen, Franny was filling a big pot with water. He looked up at me and hesitated for a second, which made me blush. And then he asked, "What's your method? Boil them alive or knife them first?"

"Oh, definitely the knife," I said. "It's harsh, but humane."

He put the pot on the stove and took a long knife from a drawer. The lobsters were trying to claw their way out of the sink, but they kept slipping down the sides. Franny grabbed one and jabbed the knife in. I was standing close to him, our shoulders touching. He took the second lobster and held the point of the knife right at the joint of the shell where he would plunge it in. Then he offered the knife to me. I couldn't stand to watch when my father killed lobsters this way, but I took the knife. I inhaled and pushed the tip through the lobster. We put them in the pot and Franny covered it. He looked at me and tilted his head. I moved my head in the opposite direction, mirroring his angle.

"What?" I asked.

"Just . . . nothing," he said.

I wanted to touch his face, his still-damp hair.

We were setting the table when the woman I'd seen dancing with Henry the night before came into the kitchen. Her thick hair was loose and fell almost to her waist. Her eyes were dark brown and piercing, her nose long and thin. In a kimono-like robe and flip-flops, she managed to look attractive, even somewhat regal, yet also like a distracted poet who had more important things to consider than her own appearance. She looked at me imperiously. "Who's this now?"

"This is Eve," Franny said, and then introduced me to his mother, Tillie. I didn't say that I had read her poems in college, or that I knew her latest collection had been well reviewed. I didn't mention that I worked at Hodder, Strike and had read the first chapters of Henry's memoir, with his breathless account of their steamy courtship and coming together as "literary soul mates." I didn't say anything about being at the party the night before or peeking into her bedroom. Franny told her about the surf and how we had pulled in the lobster trap. She lifted the lid on the pot. "You know, technically, you're poachers."

Franny shook his head. "Nah, these little lobsters were children lost in the storm."

"We're not really thieves, are we?" I asked.

"Your secret's safe with me," Tillie said, opening the refrigerator and bending down to reach for something in the back. "Here, you can christen your bounty with this."

She stood up and held out a black bottle. "Freixenet," she said. "You drink, don't you?"

"Of course."

"Good girl."

She handed the bottle to Franny and put two wineglasses on the table. She said she and Henry were going to work for another few hours and have dinner in Provincetown at Napi's. I wanted to know what they were writing and if they took turns reading their drafts aloud. Did they share an office, sit side by side?

Tillie left, and Franny poured the champagne.

"To the ocean," he said, handing me a glass.

"To the ocean."

I took a big sip. Then another. We ate sweet Portuguese bread, ripping chunks off a round loaf, until our lobsters turned bright red. The champagne tickled my tongue and rippled to my head. The lobsters were small and their meat was sweet and juicy. We tossed the shells into a metal bowl that sat between us on the table. It got darker in the kitchen, but we didn't turn on the lights.

Franny wanted to know what I loved about my job. I told him there wasn't much.

"I am a very educated typist," I said.

"So why do you do it?"

I told him about my leap into publishing after graduation, how excited I was to learn the magic of making books and how hopeful I'd been that working with real authors and editors would give me back some of the confidence in my own writing that I'd lost in the midst of so many talented writers at school.

"Were they really that good?" Franny asked.

"They were. Prolific too. And arrogant. They carried themselves like writers with a capital W. I'm sure you had the type at art school—straight guys who wear eyeliner. Everyone seemed so sure of themselves. It was like they were preparing to become the 'voices of their generation' and I was struggling to clear my throat."

When I was hired as an editorial secretary at Hodder, Strike, I felt as though I'd won the lottery instead of a $13,700 annual salary that was barely enough to cover my rent in the cramped and dark one-bedroom apartment on upper Broadway that I shared with a former classmate named Annie. An assistant account executive at McCann Erickson, Annie kept trying to convince me to join her for "more money and better parties," but for at least my first year at Hodder, Strike, I had loved my job.

"It was a thrill to read every submission, to open every box of new books. I thought my instincts had been right and that working at a publishing house really would help me start writing again. But over time, being among people whose job was to judge books had the opposite effect."

I told Franny how Ron Ingot, the editorial assistant who was one rung above me, also working for Malcolm Wing, had a daily ritual of skewering submissions he didn't like. We all laughed at his pithy critiques, but they left me feeling a little queasy, as if I'd authored the novels myself.

"What would this Ronny-boy say?" Franny asked.

"Well, he faulted one manuscript for its 'pitiful irrelevance' and took another author to task for the 'circuitous exploration of her destitute imagination.'"

"Ouch."

It turned out that reading and making fun of the slush pile, all the manuscripts sent in by hopeful writers with no connections, was not a confidence booster. Every line I wrote, I imagined Ron reading and saying, "Hey, everyone, listen to this doozy."

Tipping his wooden chair back and letting it balance on two legs, Franny asked me to tell him more about the slush pile. He pretended to be shocked to find out it was not a literal pile, just shelves of manuscripts, each a stack of papers in a cardboard box.

"No pile? That's terrible!" he said. "The manuscripts should be tossed into a pile, a huge messy pile of manuscripts. A mountain of dreams."

"Very boring dreams," I said. "Few are well written."

"Who cares? I don't want to read them, I want to photograph them. I want to take a whole series of photographs of the Hodder, Strike slush pile."

"Which isn't a pile."

"I would photograph the pile from below, to show how big it is, how unlikely the climb out of obscurity, but close enough to see some of the titles, the hundreds of stories that need to be told."

"They may need to be told, but trust me, most of them don't need to be read."

"No—better. I'll photograph you bending down to pick up one lucky manuscript. Or you'll be sitting on the floor in the middle of the pile—I know, I know it's not a pile, but we'll make it a pile—and you'll be looking down, your face hidden, reading."

I loved that he wanted to photograph me. I was astonished, yet again, by the ease with which he floated his ideas, and how pleased he was with them.

"Next time I'm in New York." And then he stood up and put his hand on my head. "Well, my lobster girl. We will never have another meal as good as this."

"That is so very sad," I said, looking up at him and not feeling the slightest bit sad. "And so very true."

His eyes were a dark, algae green. I willed myself to hold his gaze. I had been playing it safe long enough, letting myself get involved only with men I never really cared to know, and who I eventually realized had little interest in getting to know me. I had finally ended things with a law associate named Brian, the last in a line of unimaginative men, and was ready for something new. Annie had urged me to get out of my shell, to try new things and meet new people—new men—this summer. I'd gone to Henry and Tillie's party and danced with abandon. I'd jumped into the surf and taken its treasure. I wanted to be the free spirit Franny seemed to think I was.

I tried to still my trembling legs as Franny bent down, brushed my hair back from my face, and kissed me. His lips were warm and soft. He took my hands and pulled me up. As we kissed again, I knew, with a mix of relief and fear, that I would follow him wherever he wanted to go, even if I ended up in way over my head.

part two

July 1987

5

Malcolm was in a closed-door meeting all afternoon, so I left my desk and went to the storeroom for a break. I ran my hands along the spines of the new Hodder, Strike hardcovers, stacked in tight, neat rows on the tall bookshelves. I pulled out a mystery with a bright red cover and opened it, hearing the slight crack in the binding. I took a deep breath and smelled the paper, which, despite being printed just weeks ago, had the same inky, musty scent of the picture books I'd loved as a child. I thought about sketching the storeroom and drawing an arrow to indicate a place on the floor for Franny's slush pile of manuscripts. I could mail it to him, with a casual note stating that the room was ready whenever he was. Maybe I would let him know that I'd be back in Truro at the end of July and would love to see the beginnings of his mural. No expectations, just a friendly hello.

For my first few days back in New York, a breezy letter to Franny would have been sincere. Returning to work, I held the memory of Franny like a seashell in my pocket. It had been surprisingly effortless in his bed. Something about him had made it easy for me to relax. Franny's laid-back manner made Brian seem so uptight and self-conscious. With Franny, the fooling around was unhurried and casual, the lazy, circuitous conversation even better. At one point, he lay with his head on my stomach, tracing the lines on my palm. "Very interesting," he said, drawing out his words as his finger moved along the bottom of my thumb. "I see you will take a long journey."

"That tickles," I said, trying to pull my hand away. He held on and moved his finger to the center of my palm.

"You will journey to a great height, the very top of a high mountain. No, the top of a tall, tall sand dune—in the middle of a dark, moonless night."

"Alone?" I asked.

"Hard to tell," he said, running his finger to my wrist and up my arm. "Hmm, I see a man. A mysterious and handsome man."

"Who is he?" I asked, shivering from the feathery tickle of his touch.

"Who is he?" Franny flipped onto his stomach, the mysterious tone gone from his voice. He climbed on top of me, covering my neck with kisses. "He is me, of course!"

The next morning, on my way back to New York, I was brimming with happiness. I liked the idea of myself as someone who could act on a whim and spend a night with Franny without needing more. I was relieved that Annie was in Toronto at a wedding. If she had been home, she would have wanted all the details and then come up with scenarios for my potential torrid romance with Franny.

But by the end of the week, I was slipping. It was difficult to concentrate at work. I tried to hold on to that carefree version of myself, but I couldn't stop thinking about Franny, replaying his words and wondering if he was thinking about me at all. I couldn't help imagining the two of us together as an artistic couple like Henry and Tillie.

Our magical evening had ended on a hopeful note. We had tiptoed downstairs from his room, long after we'd heard his parents come home from dinner and settle in for the night. Franny loaded my bicycle into the back of his mother's old station wagon and drove me home. We stood for a moment by the car. I could see the moon over the top of the oak tree that my parents kept trimming to restore their neighbors' view of the harbor. Franny put his hands on my shoulders and kissed me deeply. In a tone that sounded definitive but later struck me as noncommittal, he said, "I will see you soon."

I got back to my desk as Malcolm came out of his office with a pale, tall man with dark, curly hair and a strong Roman nose. He looked a few years older than me, but had the mannerisms of someone younger, his hands shoved deep into his jeans pockets as he chewed his lip. I knew before Malcolm said anything that this must be Jeremy Grand, who had written a novel about a love affair in a leper colony. I hadn't read the manuscript yet, but Malcolm had told me he'd fallen for it immediately and made a quick offer to publish it. I stood up to shake Jeremy's hand, but he kept his hands in his pockets. He dropped his chin at me, as if we had met before.

In a vaguely British accent that belied his West Virginia origins, Malcolm said, "Jeremy tells me that he's recently discovered you know a gentleman friend of his, the progeny of one of our esteemed authors."

"Yeah," Jeremy said, with a smirk. "I hear you know Franny Grey."

The way he said it made me wonder how much Franny had told him. I felt my cheeks flush.

"I met Franny in Cape Cod."

It sounded like a ridiculously simple sentence for something that had taken up so much of my thoughts for the past week.

"So I heard," Jeremy said. "I spoke to him Monday before he left for Maine with Lil."

"Lil?"

I guessed the answer before Jeremy said it: Lil was Franny's girlfriend.

"Oh, right," I said, although I could tell Jeremy knew it was the first I was hearing of Lil. My heart pounded. Franny hadn't given any indication that there was a Lil, but neither had he said there wasn't. I had been no more forthcoming. Were he to discover I had a boyfriend, he could have been just as surprised. But with no attachments to speak of, the existence of Lil made me feel foolish and angry.

What had Franny told Jeremy? That I'd thrown myself at him pathetically? Had he described our time together as a convenient seduction while his girlfriend was away?

Malcolm threw an arm around Jeremy and said, "OK, children, enough 'do you know so-and-so.' It's full-moon drinks tonight, and I command you to follow me downstairs."

A tall, bald, dapper man with plump and rosy cheeks, Malcolm had a playful sense of humor and loved to banter with Hodder, Strike's much younger editorial secretaries and assistants. Every month or so, he took a bunch of us for drinks at the Guardsman, a few blocks down Lexington at Thirty-Fourth Street. With bar food, darts, and tall wooden booths, the pub was not the kind of place Malcolm would ever take an older author for lunch—for that he favored Le Périgord—but he seemed to enjoy catching up on gossip and sipping dry vermouth while we put as many beers on his tab as we could manage in an hour or so. I loved talking with Malcolm, especially after he returned from a trip to his "beloved Britannia" and would tell me about having tea with his "dearest of friends" Frances Partridge, who was eighty-seven and the author of one of my favorite books, *Love in Bloomsbury: Memories*.

I followed Malcolm and Jeremy and a few others to the elevator and down to the Guardsman. When we were settled with drinks, Malcolm smoothed his silk Hermès tie, lifted his glass, and proposed a toast to Jeremy, whom the other assistants watched with varying degrees of envy. Jeremy lifted his mug and quickly downed nearly half of it. I must have been staring because he quickly put his mug back on the table.

"What—was I not supposed to drink?" He spoke directly to me, without a hint of friendliness.

"Technically, no. Not when you're the one being toasted."

"Right. Thanks for the etiquette lesson." Jeremy picked up his mug and finished the rest of his beer in one swallow.

When Malcolm went to get another pitcher for the table, I asked Jeremy how he knew Franny. Their friendship made little sense to me. Where Franny was all lightness and warmth, Jeremy seemed dark and cynical.

"Boarding school at Choate. Freshman year," Jeremy said.

"Roommates?"

He shook his head. "More like partners in crime."

"What'd you do?"

"Pot, Quaaludes, busting curfew—the usual overprivileged adolescent shit."

"It hardly sounds criminal," I said.

"What'd you do in high school, write in pen in the margins of a school copy of *Wuthering Heights*?"

"Ink in a book? Never," I said.

"Dare a controversial new design for the yearbook?"

"Literary magazine."

Franny and Jeremy together still perplexed me. Jeremy struck me as a quintessential prep-school snob who had already sized me up and judged me harshly as the suburban public school girl I was.

I asked Jeremy if he'd ever been to Franny's place in Truro.

"Been there? I practically lived there. Had my best vacations there. Thanksgivings too."

He said this as if it were a badge of honor, and a claiming of territory. No wonder Jeremy seemed so full of himself; he was part of that literary world.

Malcolm slid back into the booth and handed Jeremy another beer.

"So, cherub," he said to me, "did you know that Jeremy was something of an adolescent prodigy? When he was still in high school, he had a collection of short stories published—a small press, of course, but impressive nonetheless. A recasting of *Winesburg, Ohio*—but at Choate! *An Enclave in Wallingford*."

Jeremy seemed embarrassed.

"The head of the English department made it happen," he said.

I couldn't help but be impressed and a little jealous that while still a teenager Jeremy had hit the trifecta of literary success: talent, confidence, and connections.

"Enough with the modesty," Malcolm said to Jeremy. "Your teacher helped because you were that good."

Malcolm was usually more reserved with his authors, and even if his interest wasn't purely professional, Jeremy wasn't his type. Malcolm's typical objects of affection were blond and droll. Jeremy's novel must really be something.

Presumably to change the subject, Jeremy asked if my family was part of Tillie and Henry's crowd in Truro. I half choked on my beer, then wiped the foam from my lips.

"God, no," I said.

"Not writers?"

"Different social circles," I said. "Artists unsettle my parents. They find them too unpredictable, I think."

Imagining my mother at Henry's party, I saw her running a finger along a bookshelf checking for dust. Sneering at Tillie's long braid, pronouncing it too girlish for a woman that age. It was hard to believe that my mother, so controlled and pragmatic, had once dreamt of an artistic career.

Uncomfortable with Jeremy's questions, I turned the conversation back to his writing. I asked Malcolm if he'd read Jeremy's stories.

"I have not," he said, a glint in his eye. "Perhaps we should organize a reading."

"Yes, let's!" I said.

Jeremy rolled his eyes. "Oh, gee, golly whiz, how great. Can we use your barn for a stage? Can you sew up some curtains?"

Malcolm patted Jeremy's shoulder.

"Now, now, enough nasty."

I didn't let it go. I was curious to know what this privileged guy had written as a teenager and if there was anything in his collection that might explain his friendship with Franny.

"Where can we find your stories? I'd love to read them."

Jeremy didn't answer right away. Then, as if genuinely uncomfortable with the attention, he said, "It was a limited edition. You'd be hard put to find a copy."

6

I imagined Lil with long blond hair, the kind that never got frizzy like mine, but curled into perfect little ringlets around her forehead and tumbled thickly down her back. Henry and Tillie would adore her. She would be a poet, or a painter, or do something surprising with batik. I pictured her with Franny roaming woodsy footpaths on an island in Maine. He would lie on pine needles taking photographs of tree trunks while she gathered scraps of bark for a sculpture. After wandering the island, they would make love on a mattress on the floor of an old lighthouse and then sleep until the sun went down. When Lil woke up, she would stretch like a cat. She would say she wanted something like chocolate pudding for dinner, and Franny would oblige.

At noon on Friday, I was sitting at my desk, a submission from the slush pile in front of me, imagining Franny and Lil afloat on their backs in a pond, when the phone rang. It was Malcolm, at his house in Bucks County, with an urgent errand. He wanted me to go into the storeroom "posthaste," find a particular bound galley, and bring it to 160 East Twelfth Street, the basement apartment.

"Do hurry," he said. "Jeremy asked for it today as he might be heading out of town this evening."

Jeremy. I had little desire to see Jeremy. I cringed at the idea of appearing before him as the lowly errand runner that I was. I looked around for one of the summer interns, but they'd all skipped out early to start their weekends. I dragged myself into the storeroom to get a galley of the novel *Armenian Rhapsody*, by a writer who'd emigrated from Yerevan to Chicago as a teenager. It annoyed me that Jeremy was already feeling entitled enough to ask for a delivery to his apartment. I had no idea why it was so urgent that he get the galley today.

It was nearly one hundred degrees and muggy outside, and the air felt thick and dirty. I took the bus downtown and walked the last few blocks to Jeremy's apartment, the leather straps of my sandals cutting into my feet, which had swelled from the heat. I twisted my hair into a bun and pulled a pencil from my tote bag, sticking it through the knot to keep my hair off my neck.

His building was a narrow brownstone. I went down the steps to the basement and pushed the bell. When the door opened, Jeremy stood in front of me with a spoon in his mouth and a jar of peanut butter in his hand, wearing a plain white T-shirt and baggy khaki shorts. He looked thinner than I'd remembered.

"Hi. Malcolm said you had a desperate need for *Armenian Rhapsody*."

I reached into my bag and took out the galley. Jeremy slowly pulled the spoon from his mouth and put it and the jar of peanut butter down on a table by the door. He took the galley, flipped through the pages, and set it on the table.

"Do you want to come in?" he asked, without smiling, seeming almost nervous.

My eagerness to learn more about Franny trumped my

wariness of Jeremy. "Just for a minute—to get out of the heat."
I moved toward the wheezing air conditioner in the window by
the door.

The room was small and tidy, with one wall of exposed brick.
There wasn't much furniture—a navy-blue futon couch, an antique rocking chair, and an old camp trunk used as a coffee table,
on which sat a glass milk bottle filled with dried flowers. Books
were lined up neatly on two long wooden shelves propped up on
cinder blocks. A pair of pink ballet shoes, their ribbons wrapped
tightly around them, and pair of light-blue leg warmers were on
the floor near the futon. A tiny kitchen with a half-size fridge, a
stove, and a narrow sink was tucked into the corner. On top of
the single kitchen cabinet was a clay pot containing an ivy plant
with wilting brown leaves.

"Is this your place?" I asked.

"Mine? Are you kidding? Does this look like the kind of
place I'd live in?"

"I don't know. I don't know you."

Jeremy pointed to a framed poster of Joni Mitchell on the
wall.

"You know me enough to know that *this* couldn't possibly
be mine."

"I like Joni Mitchell," I said.

"Of course you do. As does my little sister, Debbie, which is
why she hung it in her apartment."

I was surprised to hear that he was someone's older brother.
From the small fridge, Jeremy pulled out two bottles of Bass Ale
and handed one to me. He sat on the futon with his long legs
stretched onto the trunk, leaving me the rocking chair. He told
me his sister was at a dance festival in North Carolina for the
month and he was staying at her place until he figured out where
to go next.

"Next?" I asked.

"I'd been thinking of heading up to the Cape to hang with Franny for a while, but I think he's staying up in Maine with Lil."

I rocked a few times in the chair, then asked, "So where in Maine are they?"

Jeremy smiled slightly.

"At Lil's mother's house in Vinalhaven. Lil's working at some lobster place where Franny's hoping to get work too. It's absurdly remote. You have to drive forever and then take a ferry to get there."

I shook my head.

"What?"

"I had imagined them on an island," I said.

"They are kind of an island to themselves," he said.

When he didn't continue, I asked, "Is Lil an artist too?"

"She would say so," Jeremy said.

"Would you?"

He said nothing, which was enough for me to understand he didn't think much of Lil. Perhaps he found their relationship as illogical as I found his friendship with Franny. We sat in silence for a moment, Jeremy watching me rock in the chair. I stood up and stepped to the kitchen to put my beer in the sink.

"I'm just going to pour the rest out; I should get back to work," I said, my back to Jeremy, as the amber liquid flowed into the drain.

I was about to turn to go when I felt my hair slip out of its bun and tumble down to my shoulders. I turned around and Jeremy was standing right behind me, holding the pencil that I'd used to keep my hair in place. He looked as surprised as I was.

"Sorry—I couldn't resist," he said.

For a second, his face appeared tentative, even open. Had Jeremy been making a pass at me, at Franny's "easy mark"?

Then, tapping the pencil against his palm, he seemed to regain his composure.

"Can I take this?"

"I think you just did," I said.

I told him I'd see him around, and without looking at him again, I let myself out.

7

Other than May Castanada, the new receptionist, who was listening to her Walkman with her eyes closed when the elevator opened onto the third floor, Hodder, Strike had cleared out by the time I got back. I felt guilty going into Malcolm's office without permission. Malcolm guarded his authors' manuscripts carefully, often keeping them even from the assistants, until he'd gotten through a few rounds of edits. Before he'd left for the country, he'd mentioned that Jeremy's novel was in the "percolation" stage, which meant that he was going to let it sit for a while before he tackled it again.

Malcolm's vast mahogany desk gleamed as if it had just been polished and was nearly bare, except for a black leather blotter, a row of six perfectly sharpened pencils, a thick pad of white paper, and a single silver pen, which I knew contained a cartridge of green ink, as it was my responsibility to keep the supply closet well stocked with them.

I found Jeremy's manuscript in a cardboard box on the credenza behind Malcolm's desk. Not daring to stay in his office,

I took the box and returned to my desk just outside his door. I don't know why I felt so nervous. If Malcolm found out I'd read the manuscript, he'd probably do little more than show his displeasure by waiting a week or two before asking what I'd thought of it. But my heart raced as I lifted the top off the cardboard box and saw the first page, which read "An Untitled Novel by J. Grand."

When Malcolm described Jeremy's novel, the idea of a young American writer setting his first novel in a leprosy colony in Nepal seemed ridiculous to me. I figured the protagonist would be a barely veiled version of Jeremy who found "unlikely adventures and life lessons in the heart of the Himalayas," as the jacket copy would inevitably put it. The novel would be slick, darkly funny, and a little empty.

By the time I'd read the first two pages, though, I knew how wrong I had been. It was not just the writing, which was simple and clear and without any of the pretentious literary pyrotechnics I had expected. It was the voice. The book was not narrated by a young man like Jeremy, but by a teenage girl with a distinctive, lilting tone. In the first chapter, she was perched in a tree, gazing at the thick vines that wrapped tightly around the branches in a way that she feared no one would ever embrace her.

I stopped reading for a moment and exhaled. Jeremy could write, and he appeared to have a heart. It was hard to reconcile his snide manner with the tone of his novel, but more puzzling, and intimidating, was the tender specificity of his story. His protagonist, Sarita, was infatuated with the son of the colony's doctor and would watch as the boy walked through the rhododendrons. When he left, she would follow his path, placing her own bare feet into his footprints, balancing one foot in one print for a few seconds before stepping her other foot into the next one.

I read all afternoon and into the early evening, until I finished Jeremy's astounding novel.

8

One of the first things I discovered when starting my job at Hodder, Strike was that the assistants on the third floor are of two distinct tribes: editorial and publicity. The editorial staff—lowly editorial secretaries, like me, and the higher-ranking editorial assistants, like Ron—are more serious and pretentious, as well versed in postmodern writers like Angela Carter and Robert Coover as in John Steinbeck and Jane Austen. We favor studiously casual clothes, usually in black, that are as likely to be thrift-shop discoveries as expensive indulgences from the parents who often subsidize this low-paying profession.

Then there are the young publicists, all female and all pretty, the kind of girls who wear velvet headbands to pull back their shiny blond hair and show off their bright faces. They start and end the day perky, apparently without a dependency on coffee, and relish their role as cheerleaders for books. Unlike the more introverted editorial assistants, many of whom are angst-ridden about working in publishing rather than *being* published, the publicity girls love their jobs and think nothing of mixing work and pleasure. So it wasn't surprising that it was a trio of young assistant publicists who decided to host the first party of the summer.

"It's a progressive party," said Mary Noonan, who had walked over to the editorial department to extend invitations.

"Politically progressive?" I said. "That's interesting. I think."

"Very funny, but no," Mary said. "Progressive, as in we progress from one apartment to another. We start at my place, then move on to Callie's, and finish up at Mindy's."

Not one for office parties, with the exception of Malcolm's monthly happy hour, I was reluctant to attend one such gathering only to have to move on and endure the awkward start to another. But I was tired of spending evenings trying not to think about Franny while watching Bette Davis movies alone at the Regency.

"And you have to bring a writer," Mary said. "From our list."

"Bring Your Own Writer. That's new," I said. Mary waited for it to dawn on me that she meant I should invite Jeremy, the sole Hodder, Strike writer who was under the age of thirty.

"You really think Jeremy Grand will go to a progressive party?" I said.

Mary looked at me in a knowing way that reminded me she was no fool, that in addition to having been the captain of the women's field hockey team at Hamilton, she had double majored in American literature and psychology. "He will once you tell him the party is hosted by the people responsible for promoting his book," she said.

"You think he's that pragmatic?"

"I have no idea!" Mary said, with a shrug. "I just think he's cute."

Half hoping Jeremy would have other plans and be unable to come, I waited until the end of the week to call. But he accepted the invitation readily, without questioning the "progressive" nature of the party. He suggested we meet on the corner of Eighty-Sixth Street and York to walk up to the first installment together.

He was there before me, leaning against a NO PARKING sign, hands deep in the pockets of his black jeans.

"Ready for some preordained spontaneity?" I asked.

"Are we committed to all stops on this party train?"

His frown suggested that he'd accepted the invitation only for professional reasons, as Mary had suggested he might.

"You're free to do as you please," I said. "I'm not your minder."

"I didn't mean to suggest that," he said, his voice softening.

He asked about the girls who were hosting, and I told him about the publicity clan, and which of the editorial assistants were likely to show up. I warned him about Ron, who had yet to admit to liking a single book on Malcolm's list. "He's skeptical of any novel with a traditional chronology. Or even a clear narrative arc. He claims that his own novel-in-progress is written 'inside out and backward.'"

"I have no idea what that means," Jeremy said.

"I'm not sure Ron does either."

I was tempted to compliment Jeremy on his own novel but decided I didn't yet want him to know that I'd read it.

When we got off the narrow elevator in Mary's building, we followed the sounds of the Eurythmics down the hall to apartment 6J. The door opened into a corridor that led to a living room with a single window, a couch covered with an Indian-print bedspread, and a round table filled with bowls of potato chips and onion dip and a platter of brie and crackers. Mary was standing by the table talking to some preppy guys in penny loafers. The room was too bright for a party, which gave it the slight unease of a gathering that had not yet found its flow.

Mary, wearing a thin-strapped yellow sundress, held a glass of white wine. "You came!" she said, punching me and then Jeremy lightly on the arm. I expected him to scowl at her but he smiled and thanked her for the invitation. I walked over to a small table near the windowsill, where Mary had arranged the drinks, and took a bottle of beer. Ron, looking professorial as ever with his round glasses and trimmed beard, was standing by the kitchen alcove, his arm around a girl slightly taller than he was, with short, spiky hair and a row of silver earrings in her left ear. He indicated I should join them and clinked his beer against mine.

"This is Kayla," he said. Spotting Jeremy talking to Mary by the drinks table, Ron asked, "Your date?"

"Hardly. Mary asked me to invite him."

Kayla turned to see who we were talking about. "I feel like I know that guy," she said.

"That's the guy I've told you about," Ron said. "The ridiculously talented Jeremy Grand, aka God's gift to lepers."

"Was that an actual compliment?" I said.

Ron shook his head slowly. "I said he has talent. I didn't say he had broken new ground."

Kayla peered behind Ron, squinting toward Jeremy. "That's Jeremy *Greenberg*," she said. "I sat next to him in social studies at Millburn Junior High."

"He changed his name?" Ron said.

"He's Jewish?" I said. "From New Jersey?"

Kayla nodded. "Yes, yes, and yes."

Ron turned toward Kayla. "You're from New Jersey?"

She gave him a withering stare. I looked at Jeremy, who was laughing at something Mary was saying. I had gotten Jeremy completely wrong. He had no more been born into Franny's world than I had.

Kayla walked up to Jeremy and, ignoring Mary, held up her hand and waved her fingers at him. He looked at her without recognition, and then as she spoke, pointing at her hair, which probably wasn't so edgy back in eighth grade, it seemed to dawn on him that he did know her. I tried to hear what they were saying, but Mary, who had been pushed out of the conversation by Kayla, turned toward the rest of us to announce that our estimated time of departure to progress to the next location of the party, at Seventy-First off Third, would be in precisely ten minutes.

I downed my beer, grabbed another, and stood by the door so that I could be one of the first to leave. Jeremy followed. Without waiting for the rest of the group to come downstairs, we started walking west. For about a block, I debated saying anything at all, but then I couldn't resist. "Nice to meet you, Jeremy Greenberg."

"I'm not embarrassed by it," he said. "I mean, it's not like it's a secret."

"Of course not," I said, thinking that it was exactly like that.

"I changed it after I graduated high school. Grand is a family name."

I wasn't sure what to make of that. Wasn't Greenberg a family name too? The actual family name? I wouldn't have been surprised to learn that the name had been changed from Greenberg to Grand at Ellis Island, but it was unusual for someone so young to choose a new name and to switch from an obviously Jewish one to another so devoid of context.

"What did your parents make of that?"

"It was just another thing they didn't understand about me."

He didn't offer up anything else, so I decided not to press him on it. If this night was going to be bearable, he was going to have to lighten up.

Jeremy and I arrived before the others at the next stop, in a new high-rise with a doorman. I couldn't remember who was hosting this segment of the party, so we settled in on the black leather couches on the side of the lobby to wait. The walls were lined with mirrors, which made me slightly dizzy.

"Is this lobby really big or is it just an illusion?" I said.

Jeremy shrugged. "I think they decorated it to make it appear large enough to justify the high rent."

I didn't know what else to say, so I just sat there, not realizing that I was staring at Jeremy until he asked, "Why are you looking at me like that?"

"I just can't figure out if you are less intimidating now that I know you're a Greenberg or more intimidating for having had the nerve to change your name."

"More intimidating," he said. "Definitely."

Within a few minutes, the rest of the party arrived and we joined them in a boisterous elevator ride up to the apartment of Callie Calhoun, the most senior of the junior publicists, who had recently moved in with her boyfriend, Clint, a bond trader.

"The next course is ready and waiting," she said, ushering us from the elevator to her front door in heels that struck me as ridiculously high for an evening of traipsing around Manhattan.

The apartment was vast and sparsely furnished. In the living room were two buttery leather couches, a dark green recliner, and a glass coffee table perched on what looked like two tree stumps. The hallways were decorated with huge framed photographs of someone—presumably Clint—skiing, golfing, and surfing in beautiful locales. The action shots looked like cover photos from *Outside* magazine.

Staring at the photographs with his arms folded, Jeremy said, "These tell the story of a manly man, a true American."

"A masturbator of the universe."

Jeremy laughed. "Did you really just say that?"

"Apparently, I did. You know, like masters of the . . ."

"I get it."

Callie, who had disappeared into the kitchen when we arrived, walked into the living room with a large oval tray of tiny plastic cups filled with a jewel-toned assortment of cubes.

"Our next course is served," she said, placing the tray on the table. "Jell-O shots!" Guests quickly swarmed around the table. Jeremy asked my favorite color and then elbowed his way toward the shots. He emerged holding three red cups in each hand.

"Three?" I said.

"One is a shot. Two is a snack. Three make a *course*."

"Are we really going to have to find our way to yet another apartment before we get some food?" I asked, looking around the room for something to eat. "I hate to do this on an empty stomach."

"In Russia, when there's no food to go with the vodka, they smell something pungent, like a wool sweater or some hair, to trick the stomach," Jeremy said.

"Does that work?"

"I have no idea." He leaned toward me and gently lifted the hair from below my shoulder and brought it to his nose. With his head bent down, I could smell his curls, which had the faintest scent of citrus. When he lifted his head, the ends of my hair resting loosely in his fingers, his face was close to mine. He looked appealingly unguarded.

"Where'd you learn that?" I asked.

"My father was born in Moscow. Learned it from his father." He twisted his fingers gently through my hair.

"Grandpa Greenberg?"

Jeremy gripped my hair a little tighter and gave a gentle tug.

"The very one," he said, letting my hair go.

Jeremy downed his shots one after another. "As bad as I remember," he said. He cocked his head toward me and pointed to his hair. "Want to do it *à la Russe*?"

I leaned in, took a quick sniff of Jeremy's head, and then raised a plastic cup in the air, eager to feel the effect of the vodka.

"To Grandpa Greenberg," I said, and swallowed the cold shot.

9

I didn't realize how tipsy I was until we left Callie's building to head to the next stop of the evening, which was in an apartment at Waterside Plaza, down in the east Twenties.

Out on the sidewalk, Callie and some of the others were debating too loudly whether it made more sense to take the subway to Twenty-Third and walk east or to take the bus down Second Avenue.

I turned to Jeremy and said, "Can we just take a cab? I'm starving."

I stayed close to him as we walked to the corner and he peered uptown, looking for a taxi coming down Second Avenue. I watched Jeremy, thinking about how easy it would be to lean over and rest my head on his shoulder. A Checker cab pulled up, and Jeremy opened the door and waited for me to slide to the other side. I flipped down the jump seat and rested my feet on it.

Jeremy gave the driver the address and we careened down Second Avenue, slamming over pot holes, swerving to pass slower cars, and flying through traffic lights just before they changed from yellow to red. "Whoa, this car is going way too fast," I said, closing my eyes. "It's making my head spin."

Jeremy leaned forward and politely asked the driver to slow down a bit. His voice at that moment reminded me of his writing. I still couldn't put together the richly imagined world of his novel with the cagey guy from New Jersey sitting beside me.

"May I ask you one question?" I said, forgetting my earlier reticence to let on that I'd read his manuscript. "I've been wondering. I mean, I loved your novel and it all rings true, amazingly true, but I can't help wondering, why leprosy? Who even thinks about that anymore? What was the connection?"

"That was more than one question," Jeremy said.

I kept on. "What's the link between boy Greenberg in New Jersey and girl leper in Nepal? Did you have a skin condition as a kid or something?"

"Wow, you are so perceptive. It was eczema. A severe case."

I gasped. "Really?"

"No, not really. Not at all. Do you actually think so literally, that creativity can be distilled so simply from point A to point B?"

I wasn't too wasted to be embarrassed. I looked out the window, watching the delis and pubs of Second Avenue pass by in a blur.

"It wasn't an unreasonable question. I mean, your novel doesn't seem to be a case of 'write what you know.'"

"Write what I know? No thanks."

I wasn't surprised that he'd be among the many writers who scoffed at that whole idea, but I was still puzzled by his choice of subjects.

"But you took such a leap. I mean, not just a foreign country, but a foreign girl. A teenage girl."

"Men can't write women?" he asked. "It's a human story. She's a human."

"Yeah, a human who happens to be a fourteen-year-old

female, which is sort of a seminal time in the life of a . . . human *girl*."

We sat in silence for a few blocks. And then Jeremy said, "If I wanted to tell the world why I write or why I wrote about a Nepali girl, I would have written an essay instead of a novel. Is that concept too complicated for you to understand? Have you never written something that appeared on the page in a mysterious way?"

"As a matter of fact, I have," I said.

"So you do write. Why am I not surprised? Do you know exactly where your writing comes from?"

I had to admit I didn't. To make my point, and perhaps to impress him, I told him about the best story I had written at Brown, about an angry widower trying to convince himself he needs no one, and how it had poured from me in a magical rush of scribbling during a train ride from Providence to Philadelphia to visit my brother. The story was published in *Issues*, the school literary magazine, and had gotten a lot of attention from the real writers on campus, one of whom, in what he probably considered a compliment, told me he was impressed that such a meek girl had written such a sharp story. I didn't tell Jeremy that I knew what had inspired me—a disconcerting one-night stand with a maddeningly cerebral semiotics major—but that I was still astonished by the ease with which I'd written the story. Nothing had flowed like that since then, which made me think that perhaps I wasn't meant to be a writer after all.

"Tell me," Jeremy said, putting on the deep voice of a television interviewer, "was there not something in your childhood that prompted you to write from the perspective of an angry man? Perhaps . . . an abusive relationship?"

"Very funny. And no comment. I'm not the one heading out

on the publicity circuit soon. And good luck with that, by the way. It's clear you're going to be a real charmer."

I rested my head on the back of the vinyl seat and closed my eyes. At that moment, I only wanted to be back in Truro, hundreds of miles from Manhattan and its ambitious young writers. I wanted to be sitting in dusky light at the table in Franny's kitchen, filled with a sense of belonging and promise.

10

The final apartment was narrow and decorated in hues of beige. The windows looked as though they couldn't be opened, giving the space a slightly claustrophobic feel. When Jeremy and I walked in, Mindy Blodgett was adding a large wooden salad bowl to a sizable spread of food that included the obligatory brie, our second of the evening, and pasta primavera with sun-dried tomatoes.

"Come, take, eat!" Mindy said, waving a paper plate as if she was about to toss it like a Frisbee. I filled a plate with pasta and salads and moved to the corner of the dining room. Leaning against the wall, I ate to quell my stomach and get some space from Jeremy, who was circling the food table warily. Mindy followed closely behind him, giving a running commentary on the menu. "That's spinach salad, with hard-boiled egg and bacon. That's chicken salad, with walnuts and grapes. That's hummus. It's chick peas."

"Of course," Jeremy said. He put some pita triangles and a spoonful of hummus on his plate. He moved over to stand beside me.

"Lost your appetite?" I asked.

He dipped some pita in his hummus.

"I suppose I have. I'm not partial to salads."

"Of any kind?"

"Pretty much."

"So no vegetables. I'll be sure to mention that to Mary so she can include it in the press release for your book launch. Any other deeply personal details you're willing to share?"

Jeremy looked at me and for a moment I thought he was going to tell me off. But then he set down his paper plate and shrugged. "OK, so sue me. I don't like being interrogated about my writing. I'll get over it. Go ahead. Ask me three questions. Anything at all."

"Three? How generous," I said. "OK. Question one, were you sick as a child?"

"You can't give it up, can you? I had the mumps and a few bouts of strep throat, but other than that, I had a healthy childhood. Next?"

"What was the first piece of fiction you ever wrote?"

"A short story about a girls' volleyball team whose obsession with a Ouija board takes a dark turn."

I couldn't help myself and laughed. "Was that science fiction or pornography?"

He smiled slyly. "Is that your third question?"

"No! Absolutely not. I get one more."

"OK, go for it." I looked at his pale face, his dark hair.

"When and where did your parents meet?"

He exhaled slowly.

"Come on, out with it. You promised."

"In 1945. In a displaced persons camp in Germany. A fitting beginning to a miserable marriage."

"I had no idea. I'm so sorry."

"Don't be. They were among the lucky ones."

Jeremy looked away, and before I could say more, Mary walked up and asked if she could "borrow" Jeremy to open a bottle of champagne. "I'm afraid of flying corks," she said with a girlish grin. He followed her to the kitchen, and I walked across the room to talk to Ron, who'd just arrived with Kayla. I was surprised they had stuck with the party; they both seemed too cool for one office gathering, let alone three.

"Are those the vittles?" Kayla asked, without moving to take something to eat.

Ron looked around.

"Where's your boy wonder?"

"I told you, he's not *my* boy wonder," I said.

"No? Isn't a book contract like a . . . pheromone?"

"It has its limitations," I said, watching Jeremy deftly twist the cork and release it from the bottle. When he turned and saw me, he raised the bottle as if to make a toast. I raised my cup of water.

"You know what they say," Kayla said, linking her arm through Ron's. "Those who can't do, sleep with those who can. Isn't that what drives you all to work for pennies—the proximity to literary greatness?"

Mary held up her wineglass and smiled as Jeremy filled it. She clinked her glass against his beer bottle. They laughed. He looked less intense talking to her, and even seemed relaxed. Mary looked pretty. She had a way of putting people at ease that I envied.

I slipped into the hall bathroom, sat on the toilet, and tucked my feet under the fluffy pink bathmat. So Jeremy Grand, up-and-coming writer by way of Choate and an unlikely friendship with Franny Grey, was also Jeremy Greenberg, son of Holocaust survivors, who grew up in New Jersey.

Was it the extremes—charmed Franny raised by literary soul

mates and dark Jeremy with parents who had experienced un-imaginable evil—that had made them who they were and had given them such confidence to create? Where did that leave me? I hadn't grown up charmed or tortured; there wasn't anything unusual about me at all. How could an ordinary life like mine result in a story worth telling?

With her comment about the allure of writers, Kayla sounded like my mother, who had tempered her disappointment with my job in publishing with hopes I might find a successful young author to marry, or at least some friends to jump-start what she considered my lackluster social life. She had always dismissed the notion that I could become a writer myself. After graduation, when I'd toyed with the idea of getting an MFA in fiction, she'd told me that "having some talent is good enough for a hobby, but not a true vocation. If you're not blessed with genius, what is the point?" Her opinion would have been easier to counter if we weren't graced with the presence of uncanny genius in the form of my older brother, Danny, who had practically come out of the womb doing problem sets. Danny was the embodiment of the idea that remarkable people were born, not made.

When I left the bathroom, Ron and Kayla were sitting in the corner, and Jeremy and Mary were still talking, now standing a little closer to each other and sharing a small plate of cheesecake that Mary held up between them. I kept my head down and walked to the door.

11

Out of sorts when I woke up Sunday morning, I was disappointed that it was one of those rare crisp, clear summer days in New York that made me feel compelled to be outside. But rather than lifting my mood, the sunlight and blue sky would accentuate the drabness and dirty sidewalks of the Upper West Side.

I grabbed an old blanket and walked down Broadway and into Riverside Park to find a calm place to read the new Martha Grimes mystery I'd swiped from the storeroom at work. My hope of losing myself in the book for a few hours, however, was quickly dashed. No matter how I positioned myself, the roots of the tree I had settled under dug into my back. The intermittent wailing of car alarms wouldn't let up. I couldn't tune out the jumpy beat of "La Bamba" from someone's boom box. The clamor reminded me of how disenchanted I had become with living in the city.

New York no longer felt romantically seedy. It felt aggressive and mean. I was tired of the noise, the rancid smell of garbage bags on the sidewalks, the aggressive packs of guys in spandex shorts biking through the park, the warm, sooty air that rushed from the subway grates as I walked by, tasting like pennies in my throat.

My mood was the same Monday morning when Mary practically skipped up to me to ask why I'd left the party early. "It was just getting started," she said, perching herself on the edge of my desk. "Mindy has access to the roof, and everyone went up and danced."

"Everyone?"

"Well, obviously not Ron," she said, absently flipping through the cards of my Rolodex. "But pretty much everyone else, including Jeremy."

Mary eagerly shared what she had learned about Jeremy. Most of it concerned his years at Vassar and his postgraduate journey to go trekking in Nepal where, one night in a crowded bar in Kathmandu, he'd learned from an expat doctor about Nepal's leprosy colonies.

"And—voilà—the inspiration and setting for his novel," Mary said.

"That's quite an adventure," I said, trying to sound less impressed than I was.

Mary leaned in as if she was going to tell me a secret. "And get this—he funded the trip with his bar mitzvah money. Don't you just love that?"

I admired Jeremy's courage. I wouldn't have the guts to spend all my savings on one big trip or travel to Nepal on my own. But as much as I liked his novel, I was still unsure whether his decision to write about a Nepali girl with leprosy was inspired and bold or absurd and presumptuous. I was shy about sharing my own voice and here Jeremy had written hundreds of compelling pages about a girl on another continent, in an entirely different world.

Later that morning, Malcolm called me into his office. I

took my steno pad, although I had a hunch he just wanted to hear some details about the progressive party—who drank too much and whether any surprising couplings came about. But when I sat down in the armchair opposite his desk, I could tell something else was on his mind. In a breathless rush of words, he told me that he was promoting Ron to assistant editor and that rather than promoting me to Ron's job, he had offered the position to a "brilliant young man" he'd met at a Middlebury alumni gathering.

I was too stunned to speak or look Malcolm in the eye. I fiddled with the wire of my notebook while Malcolm, who had never been anything but complimentary about my work and "perennial good cheer," justified his decision by pointing to what he suspected was my "creeping ambivalence" about a long-term career at Hodder, Strike. It was true that I had soured on the idea of becoming an editor while also writing on the side. It wasn't only the competitive atmosphere that put me off, but also the glacial pace of publishing and the need to scrutinize fiction rather than just get lost in it. But the fact that Malcolm had picked up on my doubts about working my way up to editor didn't make it any less hurtful that I'd been passed over.

Back at my desk, I slipped on the headphones of my Dictaphone and pretended to take notes so that no one would talk to me. I was too upset, convinced that being denied the editorial assistant position was equivalent to being demoted. An hour later, when I met the Middlebury wunderkind, Charlie Rhenquist, I understood that in addition to an uncomplicated eagerness to make a career in publishing, the position apparently required attributes I did not possess: an appealingly lanky male body, smooth golden hair, deep-set blue eyes, glowing references from a summer writing program at Bread Loaf, and enough WASPy self-assurance to wear shiny brown loafers without socks or irony.

I considered quitting on the spot, but knew that the only other jobs I was qualified for were similar positions at other publishing houses. The thought of pursuing the same track somewhere else felt weighty and uninspiring. The truth was, the business of publishing had not complemented my love of books or inspired me to write. Bookstores, once welcoming havens, no longer offered a sense of discovery. Even at my beloved Burlington Book Shop on Madison Avenue, where a sales clerk named Dot never failed to introduce me to "forgotten gems" like *A Wreath for the Enemy*, the anticipation with which I entered the store would quickly fade. Looking over the stacks of new hardcovers in the window and on the display tables, I would realize with a sinking feeling that I had either read them already as advance copies or knew everything about them. It was difficult to get swept up in the thrill of a new book when I was privy to the uninspiring stories behind them: the writer's excessive cocaine use; the rave blurbs a famous author gave to a young novelist he had seduced in an MFA program; negotiations on an advance that had nearly broken down because an emotional agent was going through a nasty divorce. I no longer enjoyed book parties, depressed by celebrating writers who reminded me how far I was from writing consistently and seriously, let alone writing anything someone might want to publish.

I wasn't sure of my next move but knew it would not be helping Charlie Rhenquist settle into a job that should have been mine. On my way home that evening, on the M104 bus pressed between a large woman who smelled like garlic and a group of boisterous teenage girls singing "I Wanna Dance with Somebody," I remembered Henry Grey's offer back in Truro. Might he still need a research assistant?

My mind raced as I walked up Broadway to my apartment. I could escape the muggy city for the rest of the summer. I could spend my days in a house where creativity bubbled and began, instead of where it ended in the slow, dreary process of editing and marketing. I could get inspired and set myself on a new path—learn from Henry and write more seriously. Maybe I'd see Franny and get a chance to show him that I was becoming a serious artist too. It wasn't entirely impossible that what had happened between us in June was the beginning of the end between him and Lil.

As soon as I got home, I called my parents to float the idea. My mother was wary, but relieved I was finally leaving Hodder, Strike, which hadn't led to either a romance or a promotion. "Let this be a transition to something better," she said, making me promise to send out applications for a new job in the fall. "It's time to get more serious about your future."

My father, on the other extension, said, "Relax, Nancy, she'll figure it out." I pictured him in his plaid pajamas, robe, and slippers, a book by his side for his nightly reading of a single chapter before bed. Once I assured him that I could find someone to sublet my room in the city, he told me he looked forward to having me on the Cape during his August vacation. I appreciated my father's readiness to welcome me home, though I knew his lack of concern about my quitting came in part from his benign sexism and unspoken belief that some industrious young man eventually would come along and provide for me.

My plan seemed like a good one, but the next morning I woke up nervous. I hardly knew Henry. What if his offer had been complete fluff? What if he was as cranky with me as he was with Malcolm? Was I willing to move back in with my parents, even if it was only for the summer? What if the job did nothing for my writing? Or I couldn't find a new job before Thanksgiving? By the time I got to the office, I was in such a state that when Jeremy called to speak to Malcolm, I blurted out, "Would it be completely insane for me to go work for Henry Grey for the rest of the summer?"

"Uh . . . somewhat insane, yes."

I laid out my case, but Jeremy was still skeptical.

"Don't romanticize it. You'll be isolated and underpaid."

I was surprised by his reaction.

"You'll drown in arcane research," he said. "And be at Henry's beck and call."

His resistance to the idea was puzzling. Did he want to keep Henry and Tillie's world to himself? Was he afraid I might replace him in their affections? The more he objected, the more convinced I was that my plan was a good one.

"Thanks for the valuable input," I said, my tone making it clear that I wasn't appreciative. "Please hold for Malcolm."

While Jeremy was talking with Malcolm, I found Henry's phone number in Truro in my Rolodex and, my heart beating rapidly, dialed. He was quick to confirm that his offer was serious. He needed a good assistant for at least a few hours each day. With the same blustery wording of his written notes, he promised wages "not quite worthy of the name" and vowed to grant me "full rein to man the chaos" of his office and his mind—as if the only thing that stood between him and future publication was my readiness to proofread his manuscripts and alphabetize his notes. I gave my notice that afternoon.

part three

August 1987

12

Henry's office was on the second floor of his house, with a view of a grove of silvery locust trees and an edge of the tennis court. The room was cozy and inviting, although disheveled enough to suggest that whoever worked there had more important things to do than tidy up. Oriental rugs on the rough wooden floor were threadbare. Bookshelves that rimmed the room were filled with hardcovers, worn editions of Thoreau's *Cape Cod*, the *Peterson Field Guide to Eastern Birds*, a three-volume *Encyclopedia of Ancient Battles*, and what looked like new copies of *World's Fair* and *Stones for Ibarra*. There were shelves of paperbacks, everything from *Moby-Dick* and *The Moonstone* to *Rich Man, Poor Man* and *War and Peace*. Half-read books were left open, facedown, on a tired-looking wingback armchair, on the small table beside it, and on the floor. Illegible notes were scribbled on legal pads and slips of paper scattered over every surface but the desk, which was the only orderly spot in the room. On it was a black Underwood typewriter, flanked by a pile of blank white paper held in place by a large dried starfish, and a ceramic bowl filled with smooth, dark rocks.

I picked up a few of the rocks, which were all vaguely heart-shaped. Had Henry collected them? Probably Tillie had slipped them into her pockets on morning walks on the beach and then dropped them in the bowl for Henry to discover later. The gesture was in synch with the first chapters of Henry's memoir, which I'd read at Hodder, Strike, surprised to discover that the stodgy and self-aggrandizing writer whom Malcolm groused about having inherited was also funny and endearing.

In those chapters, Henry described how he and Tillie had begun exchanging gifts after they'd met at a party in Greenwich Village in 1959. Henry lived on the Upper West Side at the time, and Tillie downtown. They loved surprising each other with pencil sketches of the other sleeping, rewritten versions of sappy Hallmark cards, a transfer ticket from the bus inserted into a book on a particularly relevant page. Henry's marriage proposal, only a few weeks after they met, came in the form of a broken necklace that he found while walking down Broadway one afternoon to get a haircut. Once a whole word, all that remained of the necklace was a thin gold chain attached to two cursive letters, *da*, perhaps from the woman's names Linda or Hilda, but now spelling, in English letters, the Russian word for yes. When Henry dropped to one knee and said simply, "Da," Tillie had understood what he was asking. She repaired the chain and wore the necklace two weeks later when they went to City Hall to make their pairing official.

I searched the bookshelves until I found Tillie's poetry. I pulled out a slim volume, *Soot*. The pages were stiff, as if the book had never been read. I flipped to the last poem, which was titled "Family." I struggled to find a foothold. There was something about a child, and a loud noise, and a breakwater. The last lines sounded important, but I wasn't sure why:

My father's teacup swallows
in disgrace,
a filament.

How does a teacup swallow in disgrace? Or swallow at all? Why is it a filament? What is a filament? I closed the book and listened to the wind whistle through the window frame. I'd been so happy to return here, but on this second day of my job as Henry's assistant, and alone in the house for the first time while Henry and Tillie were in Orleans, I felt as if I didn't speak its language.

My first day had started awkwardly. I arrived hot and sweaty, having ridden my bicycle. Ushering me into his office, Henry apologized that he didn't have a proper place for me to work. At least for now, I'd have to make do with sitting in the wingback chair by the window and using a small wooden side table as a desk. "I wanted to put you downstairs at the writing table in the living room alcove, as I've done with assistants in the past, but Tillie wouldn't have it," he said, glancing at my damp shirt, which I was flapping against my stomach in a vain attempt to stop sweating. Running his hand through his hair, he explained that Tillie's office was off the kitchen, but she'd taken to writing in the dining room, reading in the living room, and pacing in the kitchen, and would find it disconcerting to have someone in close proximity.

"And you won't mind?" I asked, surprised that we'd be working in the same room.

"Mind?" he said, looking amused. "I don't expect you'll pose a problem—unless, of course, you hum while you work?"

"Not that I'm aware of."

"Crack your knuckles?"

I shuddered. "Never."

"Chew gum?"

I had a pack of Wrigley's in my pocket.

"Only in the privacy of my own home."

He let out a hearty "Ha!" and said, "I knew we'd get along just fine."

Henry's charming playfulness had relieved my early-morning jitters that taking this job had been a big mistake.

Handing me a thick sheaf of paper and a pile of index cards, Henry asked me to summarize the handwritten notes he had gathered for a two-part article he was planning to write on the construction of the Cape Cod Canal. He also asked me to go through some Army Corps of Engineers documents and make a timeline of key events.

The material was dry, but I appreciated the weight of it and lost myself in details about dredging and debris disposal. While I worked, Henry clacked away on his typewriter until he was interrupted by a phone call from a fact-checker reviewing a "Talk" piece about the Truro harbormaster. It went smoothly until they began discussing the correct term for the water just before the tide changes from incoming to outgoing. Henry had written "dead tide," while the fact-checker was arguing for "stand of tide." My father was an avid fisherman, and I knew they were both wrong. Uncertain if I should chime in but sitting so close it was impossible to pretend that I wasn't listening, I whispered, "It's slack tide." Henry's face lit up, as if I'd jogged his memory and returned to him the phrase he'd wanted all along. It was a small, insignificant thing, but it lifted my spirits to give Henry two of the words that would eventually appear under his byline in *The New Yorker*.

Arriving on my second day, I was disappointed to find a note saying that Henry and Tillie would be out all day, and that

I should continue summarizing his notes and do some filing. Alone in the house, I worked quickly, surprised to learn that the dynamo industrialist who financed the Cape Cod canal, August Belmont, Jr., had also built New York City's first subway. I sorted through the papers to be filed. They were disappointingly dull—royalty statements, invoices, check stubs, a few letters from Malcolm that I had typed myself, and a few of my notes to Henry. I was flattered that he considered them worthy of being kept, though they were probably just documentation for the second half of his memoirs.

When I finished my work, I sat at Henry's desk and rested my fingers on the keys of his old typewriter, imagining banging out the beginning of a short story. Feeling a little guilty, I opened the middle drawer, hoping to find something interesting. But there were no love letters or a diary, just a jumble of things you'd expect to find in an old desk—paper clips, loose change, pencils, and a few cards for local businesses, the Top Mast Resort and Cap'n Josie's restaurant.

I walked down the hall and into Franny's room. Without his clothes and sketches and paints strewn around artistically, it seemed more of a child's room than when I had been there before. A faded patchwork quilt was folded at the end of the wooden bed, which I noticed now was a trundle. The shelves above his small desk held remnants of a boyhood by the sea: a dried-up horseshoe crab, half a clamshell, a slingshot, and a framed photograph of a young Franny standing in front of a bucket holding a clam rake and looking devilishly pleased with himself.

I opened the desk drawer and found some cassette tapes: Elvis Costello and the Rolling Stones, a few musicians I hadn't heard of, and some rolling papers. I sifted through a small stack of old photographs of Franny as a teenager, looking more hippie than preppy. In one photo, presumably at Choate, Franny was carrying Jeremy on his shoulders, slightly off-kilter, as though they were about to fall. Franny looked carefree and mischievous—as if boarding school presented a glorious abundance of rules to break. From their expressions, I could imagine the whoop of laughter before they tumbled to the ground. Jeremy, with long, messy hair, looked lighter, without the serious air he carried now. I envied their ease with each other.

I heard a car pull up the gravel driveway and a door slam. I quickly put the photographs back. Out the window, I saw a pickup truck in the driveway. I walked to the top of the stairs and peered down to the first floor. "Hello?"

I heard footsteps, and then saw a young woman holding a large pile of spiral notebooks enter the front hall. She was tall and chicly thin. Her dark hair was severe, nearly as short as a crew cut. She wore a black tank top and green painter's pants and a silver ear cuff. With dark eyes and delicate features, her face was feminine and pretty, although her expression was stern. I guessed she was only a few years older than me, although I didn't think I would ever look so deliberate.

She glanced up at me.

"And you are who?"

"I'm Henry's assistant, Eve."

I walked down the steps and put out my hand to shake hers. She looked down at the notebooks she was holding to indicate the foolishness of my gesture. She swung them around and stacked them on her hip, holding them with one hand, but still did not offer the other hand for me to shake.

"How'd he find you?" she said.

"Hodder, Strike," I said, and then added, in an attempt to impress her, "And I'm a friend of Franny's."

"Are you now?" she said, in a mannered voice. I fingered the frayed edges of the zippered purple Cape Cod sweatshirt I had grabbed that morning on the way out of the house. "It's kind of refreshing how much you don't look the part."

I didn't know if she meant that I didn't look like a friend of Franny's or like any of Henry's previous assistants. Either way, I was sure it wasn't a compliment. I mustered up the courage to ask what she was doing there.

"I'm Lane Baxter," she said. "Daughter of Eric."

I wasn't sure why she added that bit of trivia. Was I supposed to introduce myself as "daughter of Morris"?

She turned toward the kitchen. "Tea?"

I followed her and leaned against the counter as she filled the kettle, turned on the stove, and took mugs from a cabinet. She told me she had taken one of Tillie's poetry classes at Yale and since graduating had worked for her from time to time proofreading, copyediting, managing some of the correspondence that Tillie didn't need to do personally, and checking the French and Italian translations of Tillie's poems. "I'm trilingual," she said. "My father and I have moved around for his art."

Of course. Her father was Eric Baxter, a well-known sculptor who lived in Provincetown.

Lane thumbed through the boxes of tea in the cupboard. She pulled out two bags of Red Zinger and asked how long I'd known Franny. I told her I'd met him at Tillie and Henry's party in June.

"You were there?" she said, dropping the tea bags into the mugs.

"You were too?"

"Obviously," she said. "So you don't know Franny very well."

"Well enough," I said.

Leaning back against the counter, she folded her arms. "He's a charmer, that one. A sorry mismatch with his parents though."

"How so?"

I had no idea what she meant. The way I saw it, Franny was creative like his parents.

Lane lifted the kettle from the stove and filled the mugs with water. She sat down at the kitchen table, gesturing for me to sit opposite her. I did as she instructed.

"Franny isn't bookish at all," she said. "He doesn't even read. I mean, I'm sure he *can* read—but it's possible he's dyslexic or something. He's not in the slightest way intellectual or interested in literature or writing like Tillie and Henry."

She went on, explaining that sometimes people have a child who is a perfect match for them and sometimes they get a mismatch.

"You know, like a guy who lives and breathes sports either gets a kid who's a wonder on the baseball field, and of course the guy will give himself full credit for that, or he gets a kid who would sooner stab his eyes with a fork than play sports, in which case he blames his wife."

"Yeah," I said. "Or like the hippie, feminist mom who ends up with a girl who only wants to read *Cosmopolitan*."

"Ha! Exactly," said Lane, looking at me with surprise. I was pleased to have made her laugh. Despite her off-putting manner, Lane was amusing and smart, and I wanted her to like me.

"Franny doesn't seem any the worse for it," I said, trying to hide any evidence of how much time I had spent considering Franny's psychology. "He's happy, he's talented, and, as you said, he's a charmer."

Lane blew on her tea.

"He's a child," she said.

"Isn't he twenty-seven?"

"Precisely."

I waited for her to continue.

"For as long as I've known them, Henry and Tillie have mistaken Franny's lack of book smarts as a lack of intelligence. Rather than meeting him where he is, which is a perfectly fine place to be, they've let him stay in a bubble. They treat him like a child, and he remains a child."

"He supports himself, doesn't he?" I asked, her statement ringing true, yet making me want to come to Franny's defense.

"To an extent," Lane said. And then she waved a hand in the air as if to brush away this topic of conversation.

"Tillie's going titilly, you know."

"Titilly?" I asked, not even knowing what I was saying.

"Yes, to Rome. In September." To Italy, I realized. Lane continued: "For a reading, and then a month as a visiting scholar at the American Academy. She's really on the up-and-up, you know, finally getting her due as the genius she is."

Lane then proceeded to give me her assessment of Tillie and Henry as writers. Her take boiled down to the "fact" that despite Henry's "epic tenure" at *The New Yorker*, Tillie was the "mind to watch."

"There was a time when Tillie was swept away by Henry, when he was at his younger, swashbuckling best, at the height of his powers and all that. But now? He's a good journalist and, in person, a great raconteur, but his choice of subjects is absolutely unfathomable. He wrote an incredibly long article about—I kid you not—crop dusters. He's a great wordsmith, but he overreports so much that it's just kind of lame."

Lane took a sip of tea. I was shocked by how harshly she critiqued Henry. His reporting from the Vietnam War, some of which was included in the collection of columns that Hodder, Strike had published long ago, was richly detailed, riveting, even emotional. And many of his profiles were funny.

Lane looked at me and frowned. "Why ever would you leave a job in publishing to work here?" she asked.

"It's a long story."

"Well, I suppose you think you'll learn something working for Henry," she said, with a quick, cold smile. "Perhaps you will."

13

The next morning, dishes were piled high in the kitchen sink. Henry and Tillie, both wearing Indian-print cotton drawstring pants that may have been pajamas, were standing at the counter looking at some kind of drawing.

"It makes no sense to put the bar table so far from the driveway," Tillie said. "It goes here, by the beach plums, as usual, so the guests can pick up a drink as they walk in."

I leaned on one of the rickety wooden chairs around the kitchen table, figuring I'd wait for a pause in their conversation to make my presence known.

"The ground is slanted there," Henry said. "Very awkward."

He planted his thumb on the paper. "The booze goes here, I man the table, I get a direct view as everyone arrives."

Tillie put her hands on her hips.

"Fine. Put the table where you want it. But you make absolutely no sense—as soon as ten people are at the drinks table, you won't be able to see a thing but who's off the wagon."

Henry sighed and stepped out the door onto the back porch. With a quick glance my way, Tillie continued talking, as if I had been part of the conversation all along. "You'd think we would have this down by now but sparring over the planning of the book party is as much a part of the tradition as the party itself. But why we start these discussions so early defies logic." She poured a cup of coffee and put it on the table near me. "Henry likes to see the guests arrive so he can be the first to try to figure out who they are."

"Why wouldn't you know the guests? Aren't they all friends coming to celebrate a book launch?"

"It's not a book party, it's *the* book party," Tillie said.

"I'm sorry. I'm not following you."

Tillie explained: every Labor Day weekend, to mark their wedding anniversary, she and Henry threw a big costume party at which everyone dressed as a character from a book. Over the years, Henry turned the costumes into a competition, insisting that a prize be given to the first person to identify all the characters at the party. The method of determining the winner was never clarified, but Henry spent the evening perusing, interrogating, and recording his findings in a small notebook until at some point—usually when everyone was too soused to argue— he would declare himself the victor.

"The only time he was stumped," Tillie said, "was when his brother's second wife dressed as the so-called heroine of that Judith Krantz novel, *Scruples*. It's hardly a secret that going with popular fiction is the best way to confuse Henry, but our crowd rarely turns to the best-seller list for inspiration."

"The costumes are generally quite clever," Tillie continued. "Ours are among the best. When Franny was a toddler, we put him in blue Dr. Denton pajamas and had him carry around a purple crayon."

"How adorable," I said. "*Harold and the Purple Crayon* was one of my favorite children's books."

"Yes, it was adorable—until he drew on the walls. A rascal even then—but that wouldn't surprise *you*."

The comment caught me off guard. How much did she know about what had transpired between Franny and me? Before I could respond, Tillie opened the door to her office and said, "You'll come to the party, of course." And then she went into her office and closed the door.

Henry didn't mention the party again that morning, most of which he spent at his typewriter working on what he told me was a "burgeoning blemish of an idea," while I continued reading about August Belmont's quest to get the Cape Cod Canal completed before the Panama Canal. The party, which would be on the Sunday of Labor Day weekend, was still more than a month away, which meant there was time for me to come up with a good costume.

When I arrived home that afternoon, my mother was sitting on the deck reading *Architectural Digest*. In contrast to Tillie, with her long hair and bohemian outfits, my mother looked typically suburban. Her short, dark hair was smooth and tucked neatly around her ears. She had flawless red polish on her toes, and her legs were a buttery tan, in lovely contrast to her tailored white shorts. Somewhere along the way to parenthood, she'd left behind all traces of the artistic girl who once hung out in Manhattan with musicians and composers.

My mother asked how my day had been, and I told her that Tillie had invited me to a party—a much bigger deal than the cocktail party in June—at the end of the summer. My mother put down her magazine and looked up at me.

"You were invited to the *book party*?"

"You know it?" I asked.

"Of course," she said. "I read about it years ago in Talk of the Town."

14

The guest list for the party morphed constantly, with names added and names crossed off. The latest version, in its usual place on the kitchen table, included Henry and Tillie's regular crowd, who came for tennis and dinner parties and backgammon; Tillie's publisher and editor; a crew of painters and sculptors who had been summering in the Wellfleet woods for decades; a bunch of Provincetown artists, among them Lane's father, Eric Baxter; and a handful of out-of-towners, including Winthrop and Tracy Grey. I assumed the latter were Henry's brother and his second wife, who had maligned herself in Tillie's eyes by reading Judith Krantz.

I was pleasantly surprised to see the list also included a few local business owners, like Bob Worthington, the owner of the Blacksmith Shop Restaurant, and Patricia Sonnenschein and Barb Green, a longtime couple who owned a landscaping business and showed up a few times a month to mow the scruffy grass around Tillie and Henry's house. The most surprising inclusion on the guest list was Dickie Compton, a Truro Realtor who donned a seersucker suit and tie every day, even during the worst heat waves. At some point each summer, Dickie would stop by my parents' house, ostensibly on a social visit, but with the not-so-hidden agenda of seeing if they might want to sell their property.

"Is Dickie Compton a friend?" I asked Tillie, who for some inexplicable reason had started discussing the guest list with me one morning when I went down to the kitchen to get a cup of coffee.

"Close friend, no. Closet poet, yes," Tillie said, bumping the old dishwasher door closed with her hip. "And as skilled on a sewing machine as Itzhak Perlman on a Stradivarius."

Before I could ask her to elaborate, she went into her office and closed the door. Exchanges like this were typical. With Tillie, conversations would often end with a pronouncement that could well be the closing line of a play designed to leave the audience murmuring in wonder after the curtain fell.

When I saw Alva's name on the guest list, I realized that I hadn't seen her since I'd returned to Truro. I decided I would stop by the library on the way home to say hello. She was my only real friend in Truro and I was looking forward to spending more time with her. As I rode toward the library, I thought Alva might also have some recommendations for accounts of the building of the canal.

I rested my bicycle against the big oak tree at the bottom of the hill on which the library sat and climbed up the cement steps to the entrance. Alva was alone—it was a perfect beach day— and using a feather duster on the bust of Henry David Thoreau on the mantel of the fireplace.

"Did Mr. Thoreau *ask* for blush on his cheeks?" I said in greeting.

"Oh, you!" she said. "What an unexpected surprise."

"And an extended one," I said, explaining that I'd be staying well into September.

"That's delightful!" she said.

But when I told her about my new job, she pursed her lips.

"Working for Henry Grey? I didn't see that coming."

"Don't you like Henry?" I asked.

"Who doesn't like Henry Grey?" she said, turning back to dusting Thoreau. "He's a charmer." She stopped for a moment, holding the feather duster up like a torch. "Charm, however, can be . . . how shall I put it? Disorienting."

"He's really nice," I said. "When was the last time you spoke to him, anyway? You should give him another chance."

She stepped down and pushed the little stool under her desk with her foot.

"Oh, we're on fine terms, it's not that. He just plays a little loose with the rules. Mind your wits, dear."

Mind my wits? It was an oddly mixed metaphor for Alva, who was usually so precise with her words. Alva, who had an encyclopedic knowledge of Truro history, launched into a detailed story about how amused the locals had been when Henry and Tillie had bought their house on North Pamet Road more than twenty-five years ago. The house, an old saltbox, originally the home of a whaling captain, hadn't been lived in for years and was infested with chipmunks and squirrels, which in turn had attracted a large and vicious fisher cat. "Henry and Tillie were so young and unprepared—trust fund babies, it was assumed," Alva said. "Rumor has it that Henry climbed into the attic with an old rifle and started shooting at the shadows. He was a real Mr. Blandings."

"A mister who?" I asked.

In response, Alva stepped over to the A–H fiction shelves under the window. She handed me an old hardcover titled *Mr. Blandings Builds His Dream House*. I'd never heard of the book and was surprised to learn from Alva that it had been made into a movie starring Cary Grant and Myrna Loy.

"Just read it," she instructed.

The book, which I read that evening, turned out to be a very funny novel from the 1940s about a successful New York advertising executive and his wife, who flee their midtown apartment for their dream house in the country that turns into a nightmarish money pit. It not only made me laugh, but helped me take a longer view of Henry and Tillie, who, despite their status as local celebrities, were technically still "wash ashores" like me.

15

The next day, when Henry got up from his typewriter and went downstairs to brew a fresh pot of coffee, I took the opportunity to look over his desk. I picked up an old maroon hardcover, surprised to see that it was *Anna and the King of Siam*. I opened it to a page with a Post-it note and saw Henry had sketched a miniature of King Mongkut. On another Post-it, he had scribbled *Go balder—with theater wig? Or bolder . . . and shave!* Henry still had a good amount of hair. Was he seriously considering shaving it all off for his costume? The stakes of this party were higher than I had imagined.

Tillie meanwhile kept up a running dialogue about what character to portray. On my way down to the kitchen for a cup of tea later that morning, we crossed paths. She stopped me, saying, "I'm thinking of Mrs. Malaprop—wouldn't that be fun? I can say ridiculous things all night, and it will only get easier as the alcohol flows." Dropping her voice to a whisper, she added, "Don't say a word about this. Promise to forget. *Illiterate* it from your memory!" She chuckled at her joke as she continued up the stairs.

That afternoon, as I was getting on my bicycle to ride home, she called to me from her car. "Is Eliza Doolittle a complete waste of effort?" she asked. "So easy to guess, but the hat would be a hoot." Before I said anything, she backed out of the driveway and sped off, her tires kicking up pieces of gravel.

Daunted by how serious Henry and Tillie were about choosing the perfect costume, I remembered why I'd always hated costume parties, and even Halloween, when more often than not my indecision would end with me in a black leotard and tights with a fur neck wrap fastened to my bottom as a tail and my mother declaring, "There! You're a cat."

Over dinner that night, my mother suggested I choose a character from one of my favorite books.

"Such as?"

"Oh, I don't know . . . maybe Caddie Woodlawn? You must have read that one three hundred times as a girl."

"Freckles, braids, and a calico dress?" I said. "Not the look I'm going for."

"OK, then, how about the young woman from *Pride and Prejudice*?"

"Seriously, Mom? Could it be any more predictable for someone my age to dress as Elizabeth Bennet?"

She pushed her plate of pasta and clams forward on the table and folded her arms. "Jane Eyre?"

"Mom. I work for Henry."

"So?"

"Don't you remember that Jane worked for Mr. Rochester, in his house?"

She smiled smugly. "All the more fitting."

"You don't remember how that turned out?"

I waited for her to recall that Jane Eyre falls in love with and marries her much older employer. My mother looked confused for a moment, then nodded and said, "Oh, of course."

Suddenly, her face lit up. "I've got it! Marjorie Morningstar. You'll find a vintage dress with a sweetheart neck and flared skirt, and you'll just need to add pumps, pearls, and white gloves."

"Marjorie Morningstar is the last character I would choose," I said.

"It would be charming!" my mother said.

The idea of dressing as a conventional upper-middle-class girl who gives up her dream of acting to become a suburban house-wife didn't interest me in the slightest. I wanted to choose some-thing Henry and Tillie would find unpredictable and clever.

"The end of that book was deadly depressing," I said.

"She ended up in a beautiful house in Mamaroneck!"

"Exactly."

"I'm only trying to help," my mother said "It's a costume, not a prophecy."

My father, who seemed to be only half listening, tossed an empty clamshell into the bowl in the middle of the table and said, "What was that book you spent hours reading on the beach one summer in high school? *Exodus*? You would make a wonderful Sabra!"

"Thanks, Dad," I said. "More spaghetti?"

My mother shook her head and pulled the bowl farther from my father, who in defiance reached instead for another piece of garlic bread.

"You're so indecisive. Perhaps you should go as Goldilocks," she said, getting up and taking the breadbasket, which she put on the kitchen counter.

After my parents had gone to bed, I sat on the floor in the hall by the low bookshelf along the wall that was filled with a motley assortment of books and magazines: back issues of *Gourmet* magazine, paperback legal thrillers left by houseguests over the years, books my brother and I had read as kids, and volumes my mother wanted to keep but that didn't fit the ocean, beach, and fishing themes of the books on the shelves in the living room.

I pulled out the copy of *The Secret of the Old Clock* and imagined myself in a poodle skirt as Nancy Drew, but I didn't have the titian hair or the gumption. The more fitting choice for me would be Bess, Nancy's timid and slightly plump sidekick, but where was the fun in that? I ran my finger over the spines of tattered old copies of *Rebecca* and *The Secret Garden* and *Sweet Savage Love*, one of a series of bodice rippers I had devoured the summer I was fourteen.

It was hard enough figuring out how to look one's best for a party, let alone choose some alter ego. Wasn't costume selection a window into the soul, a clue to a person's fantasy self? What else to make of those girls at costume parties at Brown who jumped at the chance to wear skimpy *I Dream of Jeannie* outfits and the frat guys who dressed as devils just to hold a whip?

I went outside onto the deck, careful not to let the screen door slap. The moon was shining like a spotlight on the marsh, where the tide was nearly high, covering most of the grass. The wind was coming from the south, and I could hear the surf from the bay. The water would be wavy and warm. I climbed up on the deck ledge and let my legs swing down and kick against the wood. I thought of my mother's suggestion to choose a character from a book I loved. I felt the breeze from the bay and shivered. The first book that came to mind was Jeremy's, and his wistful, lonely leper.

16

The phone rang at seven the next morning, interrupting my chance to sleep late on my first Saturday since I'd started working for Henry. I didn't have to pick up the receiver to know it would be Danny, and that he'd be calling for one of two reasons: to report on some new mathematical breakthrough that my parents and I would assume was impressively significant without understanding why, or to seek reassurance that despite a less-than-perfect score on an exam or a classmate's exceptional performance in class, he was not a failure. My parents' constant readiness to reassure Danny of his brilliance was not just a reflection of their desire for him to be happy but a force of habit. Praised for his intellect since he was a toddler, Danny had only one rubric by which to judge himself.

Growing up, and through high school, his tantrums were legendary—notebooks shredded, books tossed, doors slammed—all because of a 99 on a test. Suffering when he suffered, my parents would make excuses for his behavior, as if his perfectionism was understandable, even the logical response for someone with his gifts. No one in the family saw the incongruity in my getting praised for getting a 90 on an exam, while we all felt sorry for Danny the few times his performance wasn't flawless. My parents meant well, but recently I'd begun to wonder if their rapt attention wasn't reinforcing Danny's belief that extreme distress was an appropriate reaction to falling short of his high standards.

Thankfully, Danny rarely wanted to talk to me in these states, which probably contributed to our getting along so well. It also helped that in the Venn diagram of our ambitions, there was no overlap. He was numbers; I was words. We had come to this understanding as children, after years of being suspicious of each other. Danny couldn't believe how much I read or how fast. Convinced I was skimming and unable to retain what I had read, he used to try to test me. One day he yanked *A Little Princess* from my hands, flipped through the pages, and said, "Quick, what was the name of Captain Crewe's business partner?" To which I disappointed him by answering immediately, "Carrisford." At the same time, I didn't understand most of his math explanations, like why I should account for compound interest when saving my babysitting money. Eventually, we gave up the battle and resigned ourselves to being different.

Unable to fall back to sleep, I climbed out of bed and went to the kitchen for coffee. My mother was sitting at the table, twirling the phone cord around her fingers as she listened to Danny. My father hovered over her. "Do you want me to take over?" he whispered, looking, at that moment, much older than his fifty-four years.

Danny's episodes were less frequent than they used to be, but the routine was nonetheless predictable. This phone conversation would go on for at least an hour, sometimes two, and my parents would become anxious themselves, unable to think about or discuss anything else, until my mother would brave a return phone call to Danny in the evening or the next day, and we would all know by looking at her face whether his mood had passed. Once it had, my father would reiterate his opinion that something practical, like banking or insurance, might be less stressful for Danny than academia.

I took my coffee out onto the deck. The sun was already strong, the sky an intense blue. I heard the *tat-tat-tat* of a woodpecker in the distance. Inhaling deeply, I looked out over the edge of the marsh in the direction of the ocean and Tillie and Henry's house, wishing I was there instead of here. Soon, Tillie and Henry would begin preparing for a dinner party they would host that night after attending a benefit for an AIDS support group in Provincetown. From what I'd overheard, the guests included a drama critic from *The Boston Globe* and his painter wife, the editorial director of *Provincetown Arts*, and "Lanie and Eric," as Tillie had said, who I now realized were Lane and her sculptor father. Even if she was there only because of her father, Lane's invitation rankled.

I had spent twenty-five summers in Truro and felt as if no one knew the place better or loved it more. I knew the way the sun setting over the bay behind Toms Hill could make the windows of the houses across the marsh appear as though they were on fire and at what time the bobwhite in the tree outside my bedroom would start its chant. I knew that the parking lot attendant at Corn Hill Beach filled her water bottles with vodka, and that the Truro harbormaster didn't know how to swim. Three years in a row, I had entered the Truro Scavenger Hunt, and for three years in a row, I had won, most recently because I happened to know that the Truro artist Milton Wright was Wilbur and Orville's nephew.

But now, imagining Lane and her father sitting on Henry and Tillie's back porch and arguing about the merits of "postpainterly abstraction" as ice cubes slowly watered down their gin and tonics, I had never felt as much like an outsider.

17

Still awaiting edits on the latest chapters of his memoir, Henry continued to fire off notes to Hodder, Strike. I could tell by the way he slammed his fingers down on the keys of his old typewriter that he was writing as much to purge himself of his rage at Malcolm's inattention as to discover when the edits in Malcolm's trademark green ink would arrive. The first response that came from my replacement, during my second week on the job, exasperated Henry, who tossed the letter over his back in my general direction. I read it, pleased to see that it was neither helpful nor artfully written. But Henry was beside himself. "Eight months! You'd think after eight months, he might have the consideration to read a few chapters."

Henry seemed so deflated that, without thinking about it, I offered to call Malcolm to see what I could do. He looked up at me with such a warm and handsome smile that for a moment I felt as if I was looking at Franny.

To have some privacy, I went downstairs to use the phone on the wall in the kitchen. As I was dialing, I noticed Tillie and Lane standing by the half circle of weathered Adirondack chairs that looked over the tennis court. Tillie held a piece of paper in one

hand and shook it from time to time while Lane stood opposite with her arms folded. The conversation looked more heated
than a disagreement over an awkward translation.

A young woman I assumed was Malcolm's new secretary answered the phone as if she had been given the line to audition
for a soap opera.

"This is Malcolm Wing's office, and you have reached his editorial secretary, Jessica Blanken. How may I be of assistance?"

I walked over to the refrigerator, the long phone cord stretching out just enough for me to open it and retrieve the orange
juice, and said, "Oh, hi, can you put Malcolm on? This is Eve."

"Eve, and the last name would be . . . ?"

I poured myself a glass of juice.

"The last name would be Rosen. I used to work for him."

"Eve Rosen," she said slowly, no doubt filling in the top
page of a pink "While You Were Out" pad. "And to what may
I say this is in reference?"

I sighed. "Don't worry; he knows me well. It's a personal
call."

I didn't mention Henry, as I figured that by now Jessica
would know how far down the list of importance he had fallen.
Jessica put me on hold. Taking a sip of juice, I looked back outside. Tillie and Lane were laughing, their argument apparently
resolved. The paper that Tillie had been holding was on the
grass by her feet, and was then picked up and carried off by
the breeze. The phone clicked and I heard Malcolm's booming
voice. "Cherub! How is life in the dunes?"

"Never dull," I said, watching as Tillie turned and headed toward the driveway. Lane watched her for a few seconds and then
started walking briskly back to the house. I turned so that I was
facing inside.

I asked Malcolm to give me the truth about Henry's chapters—was there any chance he would get to them this summer?

Lane walked right by me and into Tillie's office. She looked at me without saying a word and closed the door behind her.

Malcolm clucked his tongue.

"Eve, Eve, Eve. Can't you put him off as cleverly as you used to?"

"C'mon, Malcolm. I work for him now."

I heard music coming from Tillie's office.

"Indeed, and we feel so betrayed. Do we not?"

Lane was singing along; it was Bonnie Raitt.

"We? Are you using the royal we now?" I asked.

"Most certainly not," Malcolm said. "We all miss you, pine for you helplessly. Don't we, Jeremy?"

My stomach twisted. I was caught off guard by the news of Jeremy's presence. I heard their muffled voices. Malcolm must have had his palm over the receiver.

"Scratch that. I spoke too hastily," Malcolm said, his voice now clear. "Jeremy does not pine for you helplessly, which would be a silly indulgence. He has just informed me he will see you before summer's end."

I stepped outside, walking as far as the phone cord would allow.

"He will?" I asked.

"Yes, apparently your mutual friend has invited our young wunderkind to Henry and Tillie's book party."

So Franny would be returning for Labor Day weekend. I couldn't help hoping that he was coming to see me, even if his complete lack of communication clearly suggested otherwise. Would he bring Lil? I cursed myself for feeling jealous.

"It's a legendary party," Malcolm continued. "I went once,

but haven't been on the guest list in years, which is probably my own fault, but nevertheless a shame, considering the concentration of literary talent there."

I saw my opening.

"I might be able to finagle you an invitation, but you'll have to return the favor. . . ."

Malcolm whistled. "I hear you loud and clear, sister."

When I went back upstairs, Henry was writing in longhand on a yellow legal pad. Picking up my research notes as if looking for my place, I said, "So, have you thought about inviting Malcolm to the book party?"

Henry stopped writing and looked up. "That scoundrel? Why would I do that?"

"Because Malcolm is all about good manners," I said slowly. "He knows his delays are bad form, and he wouldn't dare show up without your edited chapters."

Henry pursed his lips and then broke into a big, appreciative smile, which made me feel surprisingly good. "Consider it done," he said, with a wink. "And thank you."

I went back downstairs and called Jessica Blanken. I asked her to convey the invitation and to put reminders in Malcolm's calendar to edit the manuscript and bring it to Truro on Labor Day weekend.

18

It was raining the next day, so instead of taking my lunch outside on the back porch, as I usually did, I settled into an armchair in a corner of the living room to eat my turkey and cheddar sandwich. A wicker basket by the chair held a pile of old magazines, covers curled by the humidity. I grabbed an issue of *Yankee Magazine*, a surprising find in Henry and Tillie's house, as it was a far cry from *The New Yorker* or *The New York Review of Books*.

I'd never read *Yankee Magazine* but I had the impression it was the magazine for people who crocheted potholders and went by bus on fall foliage tours. I flipped through the pages, reading the captions on a spread about the covered bridges of the Connecticut valley and on the photographs accompanying a long profile of a straight-jawed boatbuilder from Bar Harbor. He and his wife were tall, thin, and clean-cut. They reminded me of the grown-ups in the Robert McCloskey books I'd read as a kid—men who wore button-down shirts and khaki pants while driving old motorboats and women who wore shirtwaist dresses to pick blueberries.

Then I turned the page to discover a full-page column, "My Pamet," by "Tillie Sanderson, poetess and Cape Cod resident."

Surprised, I flipped back to the cover of the magazine, which was from September 1982. When I gathered the rest of the magazines from the basket and stacked them on my lap, I discovered they were all from the early eighties and that each featured a column by Tillie. The oldest was from May 1980. I decided to start there.

I was immediately taken with the tone of the writing, which was as accessible as Tillie's poems were not. The first column described a spring walk along the abandoned railroad track from the Corn Hill Beach parking lot to Pamet Harbor. Layered in with Tillie's descriptions of walking through the scratchy wildflowers, the water of the incoming tide sparkling "bright and cold" as it flowed between the rocks of the jetty, were reminiscences— snippets, really—of Tillie's childhood, far from the ocean in a tough, working-class neighborhood in Scranton, Pennsylvania.

In clear, beautiful prose, each column chronicled a single walk—down Ballston Beach to Brush Hollow, through the cranberry bog to the ocean, out by the cemetery off Old County Road—and each column revealed a little more of the hard life Tillie had left behind. A father who couldn't hold down a job, a mother who reserved her scant affections for her sons. An "unimaginative" family whose reading rarely extended further than the comics pages of the *Scranton Tribune* or *Reader's Digest* and who scoffed at Tillie's interest in poetry. The escape of a scholarship to Bryn Mawr College and a move to Manhattan.

An hour later, I had finished the columns. My turkey sandwich half-eaten, I sat in the empty living room, the pile of magazines in my lap, marveling at how Tillie had managed to put into words so much of what I loved about being in Truro. She described how the splendor made her—and me—feel closer to believing that our futures would be as magnificent as the landscape around us. She wrote with a lover's eye for detail about "the throaty roar of the sea," the tumble of foam when the waves rolled in, the barely noticeable scent of a slick of blue fish approaching the shore.

I returned the stack of magazines to the wicker basket and listened to the rain drumming on the roof. Tillie seemed to have grown used to my presence in that she often didn't feel compelled to acknowledge my existence. When we crossed paths in the kitchen while she was pouring herself a cup of coffee or grabbing a handful of the almonds she kept in a bowl in the refrigerator, more often than not she didn't say a word. Her columns, though, renewed my hope that we might find common ground.

19

Right before leaving that afternoon, I finally got up the nerve to ask Tillie about her columns. I found her rooting around in the armoire by the front door, mumbling about what a mess it was. I asked if she needed help. Without taking her head out, she said, "Only if you can conjure a goddamn umbrella." I'd seen one that morning outside the kitchen door and went and got it.

"Here you go," I said.

She turned toward me, saw the umbrella, and sighed, as if the whole search had exhausted her. "Thank you."

Then, forgetting all the subtler ways I had considered starting this conversation, I said, "I love your columns in *Yankee Magazine.*"

Tillie seemed caught off guard. She looked at me inquisitively, as if, for once, she was interested in what I had to say.

"I love the way you write about the landscape not only as an object of beauty, but as a reflection—a confirmation, even—of your inner life."

"Thank you," Tillie said. "That's a lovely compliment."

She pulled a raincoat from the armoire and shook it out.

"It's something I've thought about but never articulated," I said. "And the way you describe your struggle to leave home and become a writer, it's like that overwhelming drive you had was part of the natural world too."

She pressed her lips together with the slightest of frowns.

Perhaps stupidly, I was not yet dissuaded from continuing the conversation.

"The columns are incredible."

Tillie raised an eyebrow.

"Incredible? As in not to be believed? Let's not get carried away."

She fished into the pockets of the raincoat and pulled out an old bunch of tissue.

"Why did you stop writing them?" I asked.

She put on the raincoat, smoothed it down.

"I got bored. Being direct is dull."

"Your writing is not dull at all."

"I'll tell you what's not dull," Tillie said, the clipped haughtiness back in her voice. "Poetry. Coming at things sideways is not only not dull, but often leads to greater clarity."

She smiled, though not warmly, opened the door, and stepped outside.

"And . . . exit stage left," I whispered.

The conversation made me wonder how Jeremy had done it, how he had not only found common ground with Tillie and Henry but had gotten enough warmth from them to feel part of the family. Had they sensed Jeremy's extraordinary talent and welcomed him as a fellow writer, someone whose gifts reflected back on them the same way their acclaim had lifted him? Did they find it easier to connect with Jeremy than with Franny? Was Jeremy the son they'd always wanted?

It was odd how rarely Henry and Tillie talked about Franny.

In this, they were unlike all other parents I knew, who seemed to have no topic of conversation as constant as the endless one about their children, no matter their age. I had seen this with my own parents, not only by listening to them talk about Danny, but in noticing that whenever I shared the most mundane news with one of them, it would be passed along to the other.

In my time at Henry and Tillie's, I'd only heard Franny mentioned once. Tillie was pulling old books out of the shelves in the living room to make room for new ones and had asked aloud, to no one in particular, if Franny would mind if she gave away his high school yearbooks. I was in the kitchen, and though no one answered, I heard what I was sure was the *thwack* of the yearbooks landing in the give-away pile on the floor.

20

I avoided Tillie when I got to work the next morning, skipping my regular stop in the kitchen for coffee and heading right upstairs into Henry's office. He greeted me with his usual gusto. "And so she arrives!" he said, looking up from his book and smiling, as if my appearance in his office was an unexpected delight rather than the fulfillment of a routine engagement he himself had instigated.

"It's Wednesday," I said. "Where else would I be?"

Henry rubbed his hand on his chin.

"On a beautiful day like this, at the beach with your circle of friends."

"I've never been one for circles," I said, opening my folder of notes.

"Then perhaps on a date. A picnic by the sea. A canoe ride on the pond, your paramour paddling as you run one hand in the water and use the other to feed yourself cold green grapes."

I laughed. "My paramour? What year do you think this is? Trust me, nobody goes on dates like that anymore. Nobody even dates."

"Don't they? That's a travesty—and a waste."

Henry handed me a tiny cassette tape and asked me to type up the "writing" he had dictated into a recorder the night before. All too familiar with typing from a Dictaphone, I put on the headset and tapped my foot to start the tape. It was slow going. Henry spoke in rapid bursts and I often had to stop and rewind to catch the flow of words. But soon I realized how much I liked having my head filled with his gravelly voice as he conjured an image and told a story. Once, when a sentence took a wrong turn, I heard "No, no, that won't do. Try this . . ." and I had to rewind, find the original line of thought and connect the new words, which made me feel as though I wasn't just typing, but that we were collaborating. A few times on the tape, Henry came up with a clever turn of phrase and chuckled in a way that made me smile, so unabashed was his pleasure in his own wit. One time, I laughed out loud and looked up to find Henry at his desk watching me. Embarrassed, I said, "Well, you are kind of funny."

After more than a week working for Henry, I had come to see how much he liked not just saying something witty or surprising, as Tillie did, but also witnessing—savoring, even—my reaction. He would say something clever and peer closely at me, waiting to see if I got his double entendre. It was egotistic but also endearing how he smiled at me as soon as I laughed at something he'd said. He clearly took joy in playing with language and soliciting a response, but I think he also craved appreciation. The cachet of being a long-time *New Yorker* writer probably was not enough to soothe the sting of receding from acclaim.

I couldn't help wondering if there wasn't competition between Henry and Tillie. Tillie's summer was affirming her growing prominence: her new collection had been reviewed glowingly in *The New York Times* in early June and she had recently had a poem accepted by *Poetry*. But Henry continued to suffer Malcolm's indifference to his memoir and the uncertainty of the new regime at the magazine. This not only was an affront to Henry's ego, but also had a potential impact on his bank account.

Downstairs that afternoon to get a glass of iced tea, I heard a conversation on the back porch. I could tell from Henry's deep, petulant tones that he was upset and from Tillie's slightly impatient cadence that she was trying to appease him. The pitch of their discussion got more intense, the words louder, while I looked for a clean glass. Unable to find one, I took a dirty glass from the dishwasher. As I rinsed it, I heard Henry's voice:

"Should I just ask, then? It seems . . . unseemly."

Tillie: "Have some balls."

"Tallulah."

Her full name was Tallulah? How had that detail not been included in his memoir?

"I am serious," Tillie said, in a hands-on-hips voice. "You deserve it, for longevity alone."

"I would rather not play the age card."

"Play the hand you're dealt. If writers are going to be given contracts with annual salaries, you should be one of them."

"That's a given. But asking? It makes me feel like some kind of tradesman."

I heard a chair scraping against the back porch and walked quickly out of the kitchen and upstairs, wishing I hadn't eavesdropped. I didn't like to think of Henry as being propped up by his imperious wife. He wasn't some aspiring writer; he had a prolific and acclaimed career. He was disciplined and ambitious, showing up every day at his typewriter to get the work done. Why didn't Tillie value that? For all her poetic talent, she really wasn't very artful with her husband.

21

I'd grown more comfortable at the house, falling into the gentle disorder of Henry's world. Unlike my parents, who could prepare breakfast, read the paper, change clothes, go to the beach, host friends for lunch, shop for groceries, and spend the afternoon gardening, all without leaving evidence of their presence, Henry couldn't get up to fetch a book on the other side of the room without leaving a trail of items behind him. He would routinely lose track of his reading glasses, his notes from his latest interview, his wallet, or the mug of tea he had poured himself five minutes earlier.

I could always find what he was looking for. I liked returning Henry's things, placing them on his desk without a word. "Miraculous," he would mumble when I presented a "lost" item, as if my finding his things was more notable than his misplacing them in the first place.

I soon realized that, unlike the impression I'd gotten from the first chapters of Henry's memoir, Tillie and Henry spent little time together. Tillie never popped into Henry's office, and he never mentioned her poems. They even ate separately, Tillie standing up and Henry while doing a crossword puzzle at the kitchen table. When they played tennis, they played mixed doubles with other partners. Henry loved backgammon, but played only with his male friends, usually Mark Graft, an editor at *Newsweek*, or Les Falcon, a retired botanist who lived up the road. Henry and Tillie were often in the kitchen when I arrived, but Tillie always seemed to be only half listening to Henry, especially if he was complaining about two of his pet peeves: the rambling ledes of *New York Times* articles or the ascendancy of "chroniclers of the rich and famous" like Dominick Dunne and brash, young fiction writers like Bret Easton Ellis. Tillie always seemed relieved at my arrival, presumably so I could take over the job of listening to Henry and she could get to work.

"Oh, share this all with Eve," she'd said one morning, in the guise of being helpful, as if she was asking Henry to do a favor for me instead of getting me to do a favor for her. "This kind of talk is catnip to someone like her!"

When she wasn't ignoring me, Tillie often spoke as if I wasn't there. One morning when Henry offered me some leftover bacon, Tillie whisked the plate away before I could respond, dumped the bacon in the garbage, and told Henry, "Eve doesn't eat pork!" She shook her head and smiled at me, leaving the room before I could tell her that I loved bacon.

Having noticed my disappointment, Henry picked up a strip of bacon from his own plate and held it toward me. When I hesitated, he sniffed the bacon and exhaled with pleasure. "Mmm, the two most important food groups: salt and fat." With a mischievous grin, he held it toward me. "You know you want it."

"OK, you win," I said, and took the bacon.

"I knew you couldn't resist," Henry said as he carried his plate to the sink.

"We all have our weaknesses."

He wiped his hands on a dishtowel and turned toward me.

"Ain't that the truth."

Upstairs, we worked in companionable silence, Henry clacking steadily on his typewriter while I took notes from yellowed newspaper clippings about canal construction. When the work made me drowsy, I got up to stretch and look at the books on the tall shelf by the window. Henry stopped typing.

"There are so many here that I haven't read," I said, not mentioning that there were several that I had never heard of. Henry came and stood by my side and pointed to the top shelf. "What would you say is the common theme here?" he asked.

I scanned the titles. They included, among others, an ancient-looking copy of *Robinson Crusoe*, hardcovers of *Middlemarch* and *Invisible Man*, an Evelyn Waugh novel, *Scoop*, an old paperback of the children's book *Amelia Bedelia*, a novel called *Zuleika Dobson*, a few historical biographies, and a spiral-bound cookbook, *Snappy Eats of 1932: From Soup to Nuts*.

"You inherited them from your spinster aunt?" I asked.

"Touché," Henry said. "These are the favorites, the ones I would want on a desert island."

He pulled out a slim paperback and placed it in my palm. *Gentlemen Prefer Blondes* by Anita Loos. He insisted that I take it. I felt a flicker of resentment at Henry's assumption that I hadn't read the book, but the truth was, I hadn't. Slipping the book into my knapsack, I told Henry I'd give it a go and report back.

At home, I begged off joining my parents for dinner at Scott's Chowder House and curled up on the living room couch to read. Enchanted by ditzy, gold-digging Lorelei Lee's sway over her hapless suitors, including one who "cannot even get married on account of his wife," I flew through the little book, marveling that this lighthearted, satirical novel was a favorite of Henry's.

That night I dreamt that I was walking alone on the beach

and came upon Henry, looking handsome in a tuxedo and dancing barefoot on the sand with a coquettish flapper with a blond bob and cherry-red lips. I was about to call to him when the flapper took off her long strand of pearls and used them to lasso Henry around the neck and pull him toward her. I watched, standing still on the sand, as they clung to each other and receded into the distance.

22

Over the weekend, I got lost in *Middlemarch*, which I had long chided myself for not having read. After slogging through the first 150 pages or so, the book swept me into its world. I read all day on Saturday and for hours after dinner, causing my father to suggest I give it a rest "before I go cross-eyed." The next morning, I declined his offer to join him in casting for stripers at Coast Guard Beach and kept reading.

On Monday, after discussing the book with Henry, who adored Dorothea as much as I did, he handed me what he called "a palate cleanser," a novel called *Zuleika Dobson* by Max Beerbohm. A satire of life at Oxford University published in 1911, it was a quick and clever read. The following morning, we talked about what we loved about the heroines of both books, the serious, selfless Dorothea and selfish femme fatale Zuleika, who can't commit to anyone responsive to her charms and who inspires a host of besotted undergraduates to die for her.

I would have expected that Henry would try to "educate" me with "big," important novels by men like Don DeLillo and Thomas Pynchon. But Henry's favorite books were mostly just plain fun. His taste revealed an altogether different sensibility than what came across in his highly researched articles and somewhat pompous memoir. The books he loved were quick to make me laugh, and our talks about them resembled the passionate chatter of fans rather than serious sessions between learned tutor and young student.

Better than discovering the books, though, was the realization that Henry and I shared a sensibility, and a sense of humor. We liked the same books, the same characters, even the same lines. When Henry remarked how quickly I read, I answered with a quote from Zuleika herself. "I utilise all my spare moments. I've read twenty-seven of the Hundred Best books." Henry joined me in reciting the last phrase of the quote, "I collect ferns," and we burst out laughing.

Encouraged by our rapport, I brought him one of my favorites, *Housekeeping* by Marilynne Robinson, which had taught me that language doesn't have to be fancy to be profound. When I placed the book on his desk, Henry eyed the title and frowned. He looked around his cluttered office and then back at me.

"Are you trying to tell me something?" he asked.

"I'm trying to tell you two things—one, don't be so literal and two, trust me. Read this book."

"That's three."

"All the more reason to do what I say."

He picked up the book, flipped through its pages. Slapped it on the palm of his hand decisively.

"Your wish is my command."

The next morning, Henry told me he loved the book, pronouncing both the writing and my insisting that he read it "extraordinary." Even better than his reaction was how his office had been rearranged since the day before. The wingback chair where I had worked uncomfortably was gone. In its place, an old school desk with attached chair and a wooden top that flipped up to reveal the storage bin. The desk was battered, with initials that had been carved into the wood long ago. There was a rock-hard wad of chewing gum stuck beneath the top. But the arrival of my own desk in Henry's office felt like a promotion, or a declaration. What pleased me even more was the bunch of wild white roses, thorny yet flowering, in the inkwell.

23

That evening, my mother received a call from Danny's advisor at MIT. Danny hadn't shown up for two appointments over the past week, and when the advisor checked with a few of his professors, he discovered that Danny had not been attending classes, nor had anyone seen or spoken to him in more than a week. Concerned, the advisor had gone to Danny's apartment on Franklin Street, where he found Danny, unshaven and unshowered, complaining of worthlessness and exhaustion, his apartment strewn with dirty dishes and half-eaten food. With my father in New York for a business meeting, my mother asked me to drive with her to Cambridge the next morning.

"I'm not up for dealing with it alone, Eve," she said. It was a rare admission that Danny's episodes were wearing her down, which made me worry for both her and my brother.

She asked me to drive so that she could close her eyes, as she hadn't slept much the night before. As we drove across the Sagamore Bridge, over the Cape Cod Canal, I floated the idea of Danny taking a hiatus from graduate school and doing something less stressful for a while. "I don't think it's gotten to that point," my mother said, her eyes still closed. "This will pass. It always does."

I took a deep breath, reminding myself that we'd been here before. My role was to quietly help my mother so she could calm Danny enough to get him to his psychiatrist, who would either talk him down or change his medication. If I argued with my mother or questioned her protocol, she would get angry at me for "piling on at a time like this" and making her more anxious and therefore unable to help Danny. As if I needed the reminder that Danny's moods always came first. I had lost count of the number of times I had overheard my mother tell someone how grateful she was that at least one of her children was "average," how having two extraordinary children would be too demanding and tip the balance out of her favor.

It had been more than a year since I'd had to deal with one of Danny's meltdowns, and the closer we got to Cambridge, the angrier I became. Angry at how we all lived in fear of his panicked phone calls. At how ingrained it was in me to be the "easy one," the good girl who never acted unreasonable. But when we arrived to find Danny watching *Days of Our Lives* in his pajamas, empty plates and mugs littering the floor and his bed, I just felt sad for my kind and brilliant brother, who, despite his complicated relationship with my parents, never demanded anything of me at all.

"Hey, Evie," he said as I sat down on the edge of his bed.

"You're scaring me," I said. He had dark circles under his eyes.

"I'm just tired," he said. "Really fucking tired."

My mother took some plates and mugs into the kitchen. She came out holding a half-empty packet of hot dogs.

"What's this?" she asked.

Danny shrugged.

"Have you stopped taking your medication?" my mother asked.

"I was feeling good. I didn't need it," he said.

My mother sighed. For the past two years, Danny had been taking an antidepressant that worked reasonably well but that would make him dangerously ill if he ate certain foods, including aged cheeses, smoked fish, or cured meats like bacon and hot dogs. My mother was vigilant about reminding Danny of the importance of avoiding those foods and even tried to keep them out of his sight. At our potluck Fourth of July picnic at Corn Hill the previous summer, she not only had refused to serve hot dogs, but had asked all our friends to forgo hot dogs too, so that Danny wouldn't be reminded of his eating restrictions and his condition. Danny had known she had done this and had joked with me about how un-American it was for her to ban hot dogs on the Fourth of July. We'd laughed at the idea that he could forget that he suffered from depression or that the sight of a single hot dog could send him spiraling.

Our mother had been just as overprotective when Danny was seventeen and it had become clear that he had not inherited my mother's height. "Don't say anything about his being short," she told me once, as if my mathematically brilliant brother didn't know that at barely five-six he was considerably shorter than the average American man. Danny and I had laughed about that too. "I hate to break it to you," I'd said, "but you're short." He'd run to the mirror and pretended to collapse in horror.

My mother convinced Danny to get dressed and go with her to see his doctor. I stayed behind and stripped his bed, gathered up his dirty sheets and clothes and took them down the block to the laundromat. I threw out the remaining hot dogs along with a container of moldy yogurt and three slices of rock-hard pizza. I didn't know what to do with the pages and pages of notes and equations on the desk, the couch, and living room floor, so I put them into two neat piles on the coffee table. Their numbers were meaningless to me, but they meant something profound to Danny. I prayed his depression would lift so he could resume the task of making sense of the numbers in a way that gave him peace.

When they returned, Danny crawled back into bed. My mother thanked me for cleaning the apartment. "You're a godsend, Eve. It's nice to have you home for a while."

She told me that Danny's psychiatrist had convinced him to go back on his medication.

"Will it work?" I asked.

My mother glanced toward Danny's bedroom, her face pinched with worry.

"We can only hope."

24

I returned to Truro with a heaviness and the feeling that I had been away a long time, that my giddy conversations with Henry about books had taken place weeks ago rather than only a day before. Henry didn't ask the reason for my absence, and I didn't share what was going on in my family. It was soothing to get back to Henry's world, and his joy at my return—he seemed to light up when I walked into his office—took me by surprise. His eagerness gave me the sense that I was not alone in really liking our time together.

"You have no idea the battle that has been raging between me and these pages," he said, tapping his fingers on the manuscript on his desk.

"What's the problem?" I asked, perching on the edge of my school desk.

"Unsolvable problem: too long, yet impossible to cut."

"Perhaps a fresh pair of eyes . . . ?"

He frowned, and for a moment I thought I'd overstepped and that he was offended at the suggestion that I would be able to help him. But then he stood, gathered up the pages, and presented them to me with a little bow like a waiter offering a platter of food.

I took the papers to my table and settled in to read. Humming, Henry picked up the day's crossword puzzle and went downstairs. I was happy to be alone. I became absorbed in the chapters, which chronicled a period of particular social prominence for Henry in the late 1970s.

Many of the anecdotes were funny, but more than a few seemed included only to puff up the persona of Henry Grey. The worst were the stories in which Henry quoted himself delivering what he obviously considered to be extremely clever quips. A case in point was his account of his response when Gay Talese canceled a lunch date because he had to do some additional reporting for his upcoming book on American sexuality, *Thy Neighbor's Wife*. Without skipping a beat, Henry had retorted, "Too fucking busy and vice versa?" Which would have been very witty if Dorothy Parker hadn't said it first.

After about an hour, Henry came back upstairs and asked me to show him what I had marked. I went over it slowly, easing into my criticisms, careful to tell him what I liked about the parts I was suggesting he shorten. He argued a bit, and then nodded and listened, at times looking a little pained. Gently, I tried to make him understand that by calling less obvious attention to his every witticism, his genuinely funny anecdotes would shine.

I watched, silently, as he paced the room with his hands in his pockets and his eyes on the floor. I thought he might be angry, that I'd knocked him off his pedestal a bit too presumptuously. But then he stopped and, with a tired but open and accepting look on his face, said, "Thank you, Eve. As suspected, it was helpful to have another reader."

As he picked up his manuscript, I asked, "Hasn't anyone else read these chapters?" I instinctively didn't mention Tillie by name.

"No," he said, meeting my eyes. "It's often not productive."

25

Biking home, I was thrilled that I'd been able to help Henry. It was exciting to feel that I was on an equal intellectual footing with him, that he had valued my insights into his writing as he once had Tillie's. Now that I knew that Henry's shelf of favorite books did not include any poetry, I wondered what had changed since the years, described so lovingly in the beginning of Henry's memoir, when they had helped each other with rough drafts. They may both still be writers, but the combination of serious, obscure poet and fact-heavy journalist with a taste for light satire was something of a literary mixed marriage.

It wasn't until I saw the Volvo in our driveway that I remembered my father had returned, with houseguests, and that I'd promised to join them all for dinner in Provincetown. Still giddy from helping Henry, I didn't even mind my mother's up-and-down glance at my outfit, cutoff jean shorts and an old Grateful Dead T-shirt of Danny's, and her barely whispered "Something nicer for tonight, please." After a quick shower, I put on a gauzy halter dress and sandals with heels. I left my hair down and put on mascara and lip gloss. I glanced in the bathroom mirror. I liked the way I looked. I liked working for Henry. I had nothing to apologize for, and no need to offer an explanation for leaving my job at Hodder, Strike. If asked about it, I could honestly say it was a refreshing break from the city and that I valued the opportunity to work for Henry Grey.

No doubt pleased with my appearance and buoyant mood, my mother didn't make any pointed comments about my current job or future prospects on the drive into Provincetown, although I saw her lips tighten when Barbara Rankin mentioned that her daughter Lisa had just been promoted at Young & Rubicam. The conversation stopped as we approached the stretch of Route 6 that opens up to an expansive view of the Provincetown shore and the tip of the Cape.

"Now that's what we call Cape light," my mother said.

The sun, glowing a brilliant orange, was sinking behind the Pilgrim Monument, flushing the underbelly of the vast clouds stretching across the sky with deep purples and pinks that looked almost too extreme to be real. The wind was brisk, and a light chop on the bay was flicking the water a dark silvery blue. It was true what Tillie had written: to see light, sea, and sky come together like this and bathe the whole landscape in warmth and color was both a comfort and an inspiration.

At Pucci's, my mother had reserved a table by the window, and she ushered my father and me to the chairs facing the inside of the restaurant so that our guests could have a view of the harbor. I sipped a glass of white wine, only half-listening to the conversation about Ed Rankin's recent trip bareboating in the British Virgin Islands.

As I handed the menu back to the waitress after ordering my meal, the hostess ushered another party to a table by the bar. I noticed Tillie first. She looked regal in a scarlet scarf wrapped around her head like a turban and a long green linen dress with a bronze pendant necklace nearly the size of a salad plate. Henry had on an uncharacteristically well-pressed shirt in bright corn-flower blue that made him look tanned and young. They were with Mark Graft, Henry's favorite backgammon partner, and a frighteningly thin woman I assumed was his wife.

Following my gaze, my mother turned toward the front of the restaurant. "Well, look at that," she said. "It's Eve's illustrious employer."

"Ooh, which one?" Barbara asked. "The bald one?"

My mother shook her head. "The other one. Don't stare."

Barbara turned to me. "That's Henry Grey? I had pictured him so much older, and less handsome. I mean, he's part of the old guard, but he barely seems as old as I am. And he's already writing a memoir? That takes chutzpah."

"He's on the young edge of the old guard," I said. I explained that Henry had started at *The New Yorker* right after graduating from Yale in 1955. "He's been there more than thirty years already. He has a lot to tell."

"If you're interested in that kind of thing," Ed said. "It's only a magazine, for God's sake, not a business that really changed the world like, say, Ford Motors. I have great respect for *The New Yorker*, and of course we subscribe. Have for years. Decades. But in my book, *Manhattan, inc.* is a much better read. More with the times."

"*Manhattan, inc.* is with the times, but it's not timeless," I said, slightly annoyed.

My mother shook her head. "Let's not get carried away, Eve."

Barbara leaned toward the center of the table and said, "If timeless means the unread issues of the magazine stay in neglected stacks in the corner of your living room until the end of time, I'd say Eve is right. *The New Yorker* is timeless."

I watched them all laugh, but I couldn't let it go. "The

magazine may be old-fashioned, but you can still find great writing in every issue. You can't deny that it's an institution."

My father reached out and patted my hand.

"It's not personal, Evie," he said quietly.

I sipped my wine, backing out of the conversation as the talk turned to business gossip. From my seat, I had a perfect view of Henry, who appeared to be telling a story, his hands moving faster as he spoke. When his smile widened and he rested his hands on the table, I knew he was reaching the climax. Then everyone, including Henry, of course, and even Tillie, laughed loudly for a long time.

I was struck by how appealing Henry appeared and how much I wished I was at his table instead of with my parents and their friends. It was hard to look away. When I did, I had the distinct sense that Henry was watching me, but when I looked back, he was focused on trying to snap a bread stick in half. He succeeded, sending a spray of breadcrumbs onto the table, which Tillie immediately brushed away.

By the time we ordered dessert, I'd had two glasses of wine and had to go to the bathroom, which would take me right by Henry and Tillie's table. I was unsure whether I should wave and keep walking or stop and say hello. As I approached their table, Tillie noticed me and beckoned me over.

"Look, Henry, it's Eve," she said, looking me up and down slowly. "Don't you clean up nicely." The way she spoke, it didn't sound like a compliment. Tillie turned to Mark and his wife. "Mark, Ilana, you know Eve? Henry's little helper?"

"Of course," Mark said.

Ilana nodded and gave me a quick closed-lip smile.

Tillie glanced toward my table. "Your family? I didn't know you dined out on Friday nights."

I was too stunned to say anything. Was Tillie implying that

she had expected us to be home lighting candles for the Sabbath? Henry, for once, was speechless. Tillie looked at him and waited for him to speak.

"Eve," he said finally. "Good to know it's not all work and no play for you."

He was oddly awkward.

"I like to play," I said, aware as soon as I spoke how childish the words sounded. Before Henry or Tillie could say more, I waved good-bye and went to the ladies' room, wishing I had walked by without stopping to talk.

When I came out, Henry was leaning against the wall in the narrow hallway between the bathrooms, hands in his pockets as if he had nothing but time.

"So," he said, nodding slowly. "You're out in the world. It suits you." His eyes scanned my dress. "You should dress like a grown-up more often."

I felt my cheeks burn.

"I could say the same about you."

It was the first time I had stood face-to-face with him as peers, rather than employer and employee. Now in heels, I was almost as tall as he was. His shirt made his eyes appear a deeper blue. He smelled faintly of sandalwood.

"What time do you turn into a pumpkin?" Henry asked.

"It's the carriage that turns into a pumpkin. Cinderella turns back into . . . Cinderella."

"And so she does," he said with a grin. "So she does."

I wanted to say something clever, but the way he was smiling at me made it impossible to think of anything intelligent.

I walked back to my table quickly, a little breathless from this new dynamic between Henry and me. My mother pointed her coffee cup toward a giant slice of carrot cake in the center of the table. "Here, we got you a fork."

26

I was distracted and jumpy all weekend. When I arrived at work on Monday, Tillie's station wagon was gone, but Henry's Volvo sedan was parked in the driveway. Without stopping in the kitchen for coffee, I walked upstairs quickly, expecting to find Henry at his desk. But his office was empty, his desk bare. The house was quiet. Henry and Tillie must have gone out together. Disappointed, I forced myself to finish reviewing the latest pages of Henry's memoir. It was hard to concentrate. I couldn't stop thinking about the way Henry had looked at me outside the ladies' room at Pucci's. I tried to remember how I'd imagined him back at Hodder, Strike, when all I knew of him were his letters. It was like trying to conjure up a different person.

The floor creaked. Henry stood in the doorway, barefoot, in a black T-shirt and jeans, holding a large cardboard box. Unshaven, he looked younger, and even vulnerable. The wind rattled the old windows. Henry put the box down by the bookshelf and pulled a step stool from under his desk. Standing on it, he asked if I could give him a hand.

I went to the box and began passing him the books, one by one. We didn't speak as he reached up to slide them between other books on the top shelves. As he stretched to reach the tallest shelf, his T-shirt slid up, exposing his back above his belt. When we got to the last book, I said, "That's it, the final one," and waited for him to step down from the stool. He stood on the floor, close to me, as close as we had ever been.

"Thanks," he said.

I looked at him with surprise.

"What?" he said.

"Not 'your assistance has been invaluable, for which I am grateful'?"

"Am I really so absurd?"

"Sometimes."

"You must think I'm terribly old."

"I don't," I said, perhaps too quickly. "I mean, I did, but I don't anymore."

"What's changed?"

I could hardly breathe.

"I don't know," I said, my voice barely a whisper. "Maybe me?"

I pressed my lips together. I knew I should take a step away from him, but I couldn't deny that I wanted more of Henry. More of how smart and interesting he made me feel. More talking and laughing. More of how he looked at me when he thought I didn't notice.

I started to turn to go back to my desk, but Henry let his fingers brush mine. He moved a strand of hair off my cheek and tucked it behind my ear. I met his gaze. He ran a finger along my upper lip, his expression tentative, as if asking, "Is this OK?"

With courage I didn't know I had, my heart beating so heavily I could feel it in my stomach, I put my hand on his chest. He covered it with his own hand, warm and heavy. His chest rose and fell. He lifted my chin with one finger and kissed me.

It was a total free fall, away from rational thought, away from meaning. We kissed again, more urgently this time, pressing our bodies against each other, my back against the bookshelf.

Outside, a car door slammed. We froze. The slap of the screen door and then quick footsteps from the kitchen. More footsteps, getting louder. Henry stepped away, smoothed his shirt. I felt dizzy, panicked. I sat at my desk and started flipping through pages of Henry's memoir.

"Henry, where are you?" Tillie was at the bottom of the stairs. "The downstairs toilet is backed up again. Where's the damned plunger?"

It was the most domestic thing I had ever heard her say.

27

A new pattern emerged. I'd arrive at work midmorning, as usual, but at some point in the afternoon I'd cycle down to Jams, where I'd lock my bicycle behind the building. Henry would pick me up and we'd head to places where we wouldn't run into anyone we knew. We drove to Head of the Meadow Beach in North Truro, but instead of entering the parking lot for town residents on the right, we turned to the left and paid two dollars to park in the lot open to day-trippers. We walked down the beach toward Provincetown and then through the spiny grass and into the low dunes until we found a clearing large enough to lie down in.

We went to Cap'n Josie's on Route 6, where we ordered what I considered winter food—Portuguese kale soup and baked stuffed sole—and drank white wine. Henry was amused by my stories about Hodder, Strike, particularly if they put Malcolm in an unfavorable light. I didn't let on how much I liked Malcolm, who was the first to admit he had "re-created himself" after leaving West Virginia, and so I played up Malcolm's pretensions, like the Anglophilia that led him to say things like "please have this done by Monday week."

Henry regaled me with stories about his early days as a reporter. I loved imagining him as a young man, traveling the country with a reporter's notebook in his back pocket, listening intently to farm folk and factory workers who had never spoken to a reporter, let alone one from New York, or sitting at his portable manual typewriter in a seedy motel room, shirtsleeves rolled up on his muscular arms, a cigarette burning out in a blocky glass ashtray as he wrote into the night. I was taken with the idea of learning about writing by looking outward—to the world and other people's stories—instead of by retreating to my inner world, which too often left me stymied by self-doubt.

I was undeniably nervous the first time we slept together, the day after that first kiss in Henry's office. Insisting that we weren't going to start off like "teenagers in the back seat of the car," Henry took advantage of Tillie's presence at an all-day poetry workshop at Castle Hill and booked a room at the Governor Prence Motel in North Truro. We walked into the room, and when he'd closed the door, I was afraid to look at him. I sat on the edge of the bed, anxiously tracing the swirling pattern on the orange polyester bedspread.

"Is this all new to you?" Henry had asked softly, sitting beside me and placing his hand over mine.

I looked around the room, at the faded lampshade on the night table, the crude drawing of a lobster boat in a driftwood frame.

"Being in a motel with an older man?" I purposely left out the word *married*. "Definitely new."

"And this?" Henry said. He lifted my hair and kissed my neck.

"I'm not a total novice," I said, feeling my face flush as I remembered that the last person I'd kissed was his son. I was tempted to get up and leave, feeling how wrong this was, but Henry, misinterpreting my embarrassment, cupped my face in his hands and said, "It's OK. We can take it slow." The expression on his face was so kind and sincere, so uniquely his. I leaned in and pressed my lips to his, kissing him slowly at first, and then ravenously—until without thinking about it, I had climbed on top of him, wrapped my legs around his torso, and dug my fingers into his hair. The look on his face—surprised, amused, a little helpless—was thrilling.

Making love with Henry was something new for me. He was so relaxed and confident, so focused on my pleasure and with showing me what he liked, that I was able to let go in a way that was both more comfortable and exciting than anything I had known before. Afterward, sprawled across the sheets, the blanket kicked to the ground, my body hummed. I slept deeply until dusty beams of afternoon sun shooting through the blinds awakened me. I opened my eyes to see Henry watching me, his expression assuring me this would happen again and again.

With guys my own age, I had worried about being judged as immature or inexperienced. With Henry, I came to realize my youth was no longer a handicap. My youth was power. He loved my skin, my hair, my energy, and I loved his tenderness and generosity. His hands on me, his vision of me, unlocked in me the ability to play the wild young thing. I had never felt so reckless, or so bold. With him, I had a sense of abandon, exhilarated by his joy not only in my essential goodness, but in my willingness to be bad.

I didn't think of Tillie often, and when I did, I convinced myself I was not guilty. I was critical of her. I told myself she had let this happen by neglecting Henry, by not seeming to care about what he said or wrote or how he spent his days. I held it against her that she didn't notice how much laughter came from Henry's office when we were both there, and how frequently we were not.

The more time I spent with Henry, the more I really liked him. We clicked, both physically and intellectually. We talked about books we loved, of course, but also articles he wanted to write. I told him about the stories I had written and the ones I was struggling to finish. He didn't dismiss my difficulties as proof that I wasn't destined to be a writer, but gently encouraged me not to give up.

We gossiped about people in Truro. He was surprised by my friendship with Alva, who he insisted was "a bit of a busybody" and "a tad too judgmental," although he never explained why. Henry loved hearing about my parents and their Truro friends, many of whom were also friends from back home in Newton, a fact that Henry couldn't fathom.

"So, let me get this straight," he said one afternoon in his office, looking up from his typewriter. "The Truro Sapersteins with whom your parents dined at the Red Inn last night are one and the same as the Newton Sapersteins with whom they play bridge all winter?"

"That's right," I said.

"Extraordinary. Baffling."

It did seem absurd, and yet I came to my parents' defense.

"C'mon, half the people who come by to play tennis with you are friends from Manhattan," I said.

"But we rarely see them in New York!" Henry said. "In summer, we mix things up. Throw new people into the pot." He smiled. "Looking further afield for entertainment makes things *much* more interesting."

"You didn't look far at all," I said. "I practically fell into your lap."

He glanced at his office door, which was closed.

"Speaking of laps . . ."

Henry liked when I teased him, and I never felt more his equal than when he teased me back. On a long walk one afternoon at High Head Beach, I suggested that for the book party he dress as Odysseus, to which he said, "Even I don't have an ego that big." I suggested Mr. Blandings, the city slicker who takes on a dilapidated country home. He looked at me with surprise and approval, and said, "Colossal idea, colossal," which sounded so absurd that I gave him a playful shove and ended up wrestling him onto his back on the sand and straddling him. Squinting up at me, he said I should dress as Scheherazade.

"Because I tell stories?" I said, pinning his hands onto the sand.

He pressed up and flipped me over. "Because you tell stories—and because I want to see you in a harem outfit."

I knew my affair with Henry was just a summer dalliance. I reveled in the attention and forbidden fun, aware that it would be fleeting. That I had spent the night with Franny, that I had pined for him so pathetically, even though we had hardly even had one meaningful conversation, seemed foolish now. I felt like a different person than the girl who had let Franny enchant her, kiss her, touch her, and leave, as if that was all she had wanted or deserved.

28

Lane was the first to be suspicious.

"What's with the bounce in your step?" she asked, as I walked into the kitchen one morning. She was sitting on the counter by the sink, in a short skirt and bare legs, kicking her Doc Martens against the wooden cabinets as if she owned the place. Tillie was nowhere to be seen.

"I don't know, just in a good mood," I said. I turned away to pour myself some coffee, and then took a long time looking for milk in the refrigerator.

"Have you chosen a costume for the party?" I asked from inside the fridge, as I moved the cartons around. I had nearly settled on a character.

"Oh God, no," Lane said. "I'll pull something together at the last minute. The whole thing is ridiculous, don't you think? I mean, really. Grown men and women dressing up?"

"It's unusual," I said, closing the refrigerator door.

Lane stretched her legs out, circled her ankles. I couldn't tell if she was admiring her lean legs or her thick boots. She seemed genuinely unaware of her looks, which was shocking considering how beautiful she was, with her dark brows and heavily lashed gray eyes. She flattened her palms against the kitchen counter. I was surprised to see that her fingernails were bitten down to nothing; the first sign of a crack in her armor. The poise that intimidated me might be the result of more effort than I had assumed.

"The worst are the joined-at-the-hip couples who dress up as paired characters—Anna Karenina and Vronsky. Emma Bovary and what's-his-name, Rodolphe. Dr. Zhivago and Lara. Humbert Humbert and Lolita, for God's sake," she said.

Her choice of adulterous pairings wasn't lost on me. I stared intently at the sugar bowl as I spooned sugar into my coffee and stirred several times.

"I suppose for the long-married, it's a turn-on," Lane said. She hopped off the counter and stretched her arms over her head and arched her back. "Some weird intellectual foreplay."

I took a sip of coffee and tried to sound knowing. "I would think that dressing up in his-and-hers outfits is a sign of a good relationship. Of compatibility."

"Or a sign of overcompensating," Lane said, putting her hands on her hips and stretching her torso to the right and to the left, like a boxer about to enter the ring. "Haven't you ever noticed that the couples that seem the most perfect—always happy, photo-ready, holding hands, and all that—are the ones that later go down in flames?"

I hadn't and I said so.

"Oh, come on," Lane said, hands still on her hips. "Mr. Little League coach is a mean drunk after dark. Ms. PTA is a binger-purger. That kind of thing." She paused. "You should always be wary of people who go on and on about writing their own wedding vows."

"You think people who promise to always laugh at each other's jokes are doomed for divorce?"

"Actually, I do," Lane said.

"That's a bit harsh."

"Not so," Lane said. She pursed her lips. "Honestly, I can always tell what's going on in a relationship. And it's often the exact opposite of what people see. It's just a matter of watching *very* carefully."

She looked at me as though waiting for me to speak. Or confess. I looked down at my coffee, blew on it as if it were still hot.

"Time to work," I said, and left the kitchen.

Upstairs, Henry was sitting at his desk. He stretched an arm out toward me. I put my fingers to my lips and closed the door behind me until the latch clicked quietly. "Lane," I whispered, pointing to the floor. "I like her, but she scares the shit out of me."

"Silly girl," he said, gesturing for me to come to him and then pulling me onto his lap. He buried his face in my hair, nuzzled my neck.

"Who's silly—Lane or me?"

He lifted his head and, for a moment, looked serious, as if he were giving the question some thought.

"Both."

I frowned.

"But in different ways. Lane is silly in her seriousness of purpose. She believes it's a sign of her maturity when, in fact, it's the opposite."

I was surprised that he had given Lane that much thought.

"And me?" I asked.

Henry ran his hand along my collarbone, slipped his fingers under the strap of my tank top. "You," he said, "are delightfully silly in your willingness to let me do this." He kissed my shoulder. "And this. And this."

29

"So you're working for Henry Grey! What's that like?"

It was an innocent question, and one I expected to get a few times before my parents' cocktail party was over, but I didn't know how to answer. I didn't want to lie to Arnold, but the whole truth was obviously not an option. A tax lawyer like my father, Arnold Schein was like an uncle to me, always thoughtful and kind. I had known him since I was four and had discovered his daughter, Tina, while our families were clamming at Cold Storage Beach. Tina and I, having lost interest in digging for sea clams, had teamed up to build what we declared the prettiest drip castle in the world. By the time we were done, we had bonded like sisters and our parents had started what would become an enduring friendship. Tina, still one of my few close friends, was living in Barcelona, which was both a disappointment and a relief. If she had been in Truro, I would have confided in her about Henry and had to hear her opinion, for better or worse. It was easier to keep it to myself.

"The work is interesting in that Henry has eclectic interests," I told Arnold. "But it's also sometimes a bit clerical and dull—you know, filing and things like that." My eyes swept across the hills, down to the marsh and, on its far edge, the narrow Pamet River, which on an incoming tide ribboned toward Henry and Tillie's house. "The setting is more exquisite than the cubicle I had in the city, but in some ways it was a lateral move." I imagined Henry chuckling and saying, "Lateral indeed."

Arnold lifted his scotch to clink it against my glass of wine. "It's summer," he said. "Don't take things too seriously. You'll move on in the fall and put that expensive education to good use. Just make sure the illustrious Mr. Grey treats you well."

Arnold joined his wife at the end of the deck. Watching couples chatting and laughing politely, I realized that my parents' friends were roughly the same age as Henry. But they all looked so stiff and starched, their clothes restrictive on their middle-aged bodies, as if even the laces of their shoes were tied extra tight. I would never consider a sexual interlude with any of them. Or would I? I glanced around, at Arnold, with his khaki shorts, knobby knees, and clean Top-Siders; Don Schwartz, with his crisp, short-sleeved button-down shirt and pressed slacks; and his wife, Elaine, with her chunky necklace, starched linen blouse, and flowery, cropped pants.

And then, with a new willingness to consider the previously unimaginable, I pictured myself crossing a line so ingrained in me I hadn't known it was there: *Hey, Arnold, can I join you?* I slip into the hot tub on the side of his house and untie the halter strap of my bathing suit. He is shocked; I smile at him to calm his nerves as I float up and touch his waist. *Don, I think you missed a button*, as I undo the other buttons and press my lips to his chest. *Elaine, don't mind me*, as I walk up behind her and slip my hands under her pink blouse and touch her small breasts.

What was wrong with me? Had Henry uncorked me like a bottle, releasing a looser, reckless Eve?

Henry, I told myself, existed on a different plane. He was more sexy professor than stiff, middle-aged dad. He and Tillie were from a completely different world. They would never start their days with dull rides on a commuter train to uninspiring jobs. Henry and Tillie lived outside the conventions that guided my parents and their friends. As I was learning, creative people, real writers and artists, made their own rules. This summer, I too was playing by those rules.

Across the deck, my father was carrying two drinks precariously in a single hand and a wooden board of cheese and crackers in the other toward a table covered with platters of smoked bluefish, shrimp cocktail, and spinach dip. Walking over to him, I caught a wheel of brie as it was about to slide off his tray and set it on the table. My father handed me a drink. "I can't for the life of me recall who wanted this, so have at it," he said. "It's vodka and tonic."

"Thank you kindly," I said, and took a sip. My dad looked as trim and neat as ever, his plaid short-sleeved shirt tucked smoothly into his khaki pants. Along with marrying a woman two inches taller than he was, my father's love of simple Truro, so unexpected for a man who looked as if he belonged at a staid suburban country club, was one of the only unconventional things about him. He was totally at peace here, where he loved to walk the beach with a fishing rod, garden with my mother, and fall asleep reading the newspaper on the beach. I shared his love of the landscape but couldn't understand why his bland social life didn't stifle him.

"Do you really like all this?" I asked. "I mean, it's like you took a complete cocktail party in Newton—same guest list, same menu, plus smoked bluefish—and airlifted it across the bay and plunked it down in Truro."

My father looked at me as if he didn't understand the question.

"These are our friends, Eve. Why wouldn't we like it?"

We stood in silence for a moment, watching Don hold forth about something to Arnold and his wife, both of whom looked slightly bored. The rest of the guests, probably without thinking, had slipped into same-sex gatherings, the women on the far side of the deck, talking in low voices punctuated by occasional high-pitched laughter, and the men closer to my father and me, their voices rising enough for me to know they were debating something about Reagan and Gorbachev.

"The thing is, Eve, I never wanted a big life."

"You wanted a small life?"

He shook his head and looked at me as if I was a child.

"I wanted a good life. A wife I loved, kids, a secure job, a home in a safe, quiet place like Newton, with good schools. Those things matter more than you think, Eve." He swept an arm toward his friends, the harbor in the distance. "All this? It's more than I ever imagined. If this is the pinnacle, if this is my life and these are my friends, that's fine with me."

I was about to ask if he thought my mother agreed, when I felt a hand on my arm. My mother's college roommate, Roz, who rented near the ocean every August, took my hand and pulled me to the side of the deck to sit down on the bench. "Is Tillie as eccentric as she comes off in her poems?"

She looked at me with such expectation that I had to laugh. It's not everyone who wants to gossip about a poet.

"She's more pretentious than she is eccentric," I said.

Roz crossed her legs, rested an elbow on her knee, and rocked her glass of white wine.

"But the things she writes about! In one poem she describes making love to her husband in a hammock, above a circle of lit candles! Who does that?"

I didn't like to think of Tillie and Henry making love anywhere, let alone outside in a hammock.

"Oh, Roz," I said, "you shouldn't take poetry so literally."

30

At breakfast, my mother announced that Danny was coming to Truro for a quick visit and that she was counting on me to spend the day with him.

"But I have to work," I said, hating the idea of not seeing Henry.

My mother stopped stirring her coffee.

"On Saturday?" She eyed my father.

"Isn't this supposed to be a part-time job?" he asked. "It seems like it's swallowing you whole. I trust Henry is not asking too much?"

"He's not," I said. "There's a lot of work to do and I find it interesting." I tried to sound casual, as if I hardly gave Henry himself any thought, when in truth I thought about him all the time. "I don't see why I have to drop everything for Danny."

My father sighed. My mother set down her coffee.

"He's already on his way," she said. "I doubt he'd be coming if you weren't here. Seriously, Eve, who needs you more right now—Henry or your brother?"

Understandably, the thought that I might need Henry had never occurred to her. But my parents were right; I should spend time with Danny. I remembered how frightened I was by the depths of his sadness the last time I saw him. I agreed to take the day off.

When Danny arrived, I was glad to see he looked a little more himself, not as washed-out, and almost back to being the baby-faced guy whose soft brown eyes and flop of smooth, dark hair over his forehead made him look more like a musician than a mathematician. But he was still lethargic. Stretched out on the living room couch with his eyes closed, he nixed all my ideas for our day together. He didn't want to canoe up the Pamet River to Jams. Or go sailing in the bay. Or ride the bike paths in the Provincetown dunes.

"How about I pack a lunch for you to take to the beach?" my mother asked. She spoke so sweetly that I wouldn't have been surprised if she suggested a childhood menu of peanut butter and jelly with the crusts cut off and a pack of Oreos.

Danny opened his eyes and, in an unusually snappy tone, said, "How about . . . not." He stood up, put on his dark sunglasses, and grabbed the keys to his car. "C'mon, Eve. Let's go for a drive."

I followed Danny outside. He drove too fast down Toms Hill Road to Castle Road and toward Truro Center.

"How can you stand living with her again?" he said. "She's suffocating."

"Me? I've been living away for years. You're the one who's always seeking her out for help."

"It's a pattern I'm trying to break," he said, taking the curve before Castle Hill dangerously fast. "I've realized she shouldn't be my go-to person for sharing my doubts about pursuing mathematics."

It was the first I'd heard of his misgivings.

"But you love math. What else could you possibly do?"

"Yup, that's the problem. I don't know. But it's not fun

anymore. It's jumping through hoops, trying to stay a step ahead. And for what?"

I was surprised but excited at the thought of Danny trying something new, putting his incredible intelligence and focus to a purpose other than advanced mathematics, the pursuit of which I'd never understood anyway.

"So do something else. What's stopping you?"

Danny pulled onto Route 6 heading toward Wellfleet.

"That's rich, coming from you," he said.

"What's that supposed to mean?"

"C'mon, Eve, you've been talking about writing seriously for years, yet all you do is dance around it. What's stopping *you*?"

"I'm working on it," I said, but as I spoke I realized that since I'd gotten involved with Henry I hadn't written a single word.

Danny put on his blinker and turned left off the highway into the entrance to the dump.

"Swap shop?" I asked.

"Swap shop," he said, smiling for the first time that day.

Danny and I loved the swap shop at the town dump. Housed in a wooden shack, the outside of which was completely covered in old traffic, parking, and shop signs from all over the Cape, it was Truro's version of a Goodwill store. But instead of paying for the items, you could take anything you wanted, preferably as long as you left behind something else. Filled with old fishing gear, handbags and dishware, record albums and books, percolators, wind chimes and macramé plant hangers, the swap shop was the realization of the old adage that one person's trash was another person's treasure. Danny and I loved finding weird stuff there, always hoping to trump our best childhood discovery— an ancient gumball machine that was still half-filled with caked and faded gumballs that we chewed despite their age.

Inside, Danny gravitated toward the crates of old record

albums, and I sifted through some bolts of fabric, hoping to find something to adorn my dress for the book party. I was starting to feel good about my costume choice, which, I hoped, would be both beautiful and difficult to guess. I was unraveling some strands of lace when I heard a familiar voice bellow, "Where do the books go?"

It was Henry, carrying a red plastic milk crate. He spotted me as he set the books atop a shelf on the side of the room. Taking a quick look around the shop, which was unusually crowded that morning, Henry came to my side and said, "Well, if it isn't my long-lost assistant."

"What brings you here?" I whispered, hoping he would lower his voice too.

"Tillie wanted me to get rid of these books that she cleared out of the living room shelves." He hooked his pinky through mine beneath the table. "It was a welcome distraction. I missed you this morning. Is it a fair swap for me to leave the books and take you?"

"I wish," I whispered, turning toward Danny, who was trying on a cowboy hat on the far side of the room. "I'm here with my brother."

"Right then," Henry said, releasing my finger and displaying not the slightest inclination to be introduced to Danny. "I'll be off then. Until Monday." He paused. "Unless, of course, I happen to run into you at the flea market tomorrow. I'll be there at around 8:30. For socks."

"Socks?"

"Yes. I am in dire need of socks. Therefore, I will be at the flea market tomorrow to purchase socks. By myself. Did I mention that I would be there at 8:30?"

"I think you might have," I said.

With a wink, he turned and left. Danny walked over, holding

a record album. I grabbed it from him. "Hey, it's the Monkees!"
I said, a little too loud.

Danny looked at the door.

"Who was that?"

I hadn't realized he had noticed.

"Oh, that was Henry," I said. "My employer." I tried to make
the word sound formal.

"Your employer?" Danny scowled, looking into my eyes for
long enough that I had to turn away. "I hope you know what
you're doing."

I'd forgotten how well he knew me.

31

On summer weekends, the vast parking lot of the Wellfleet Drive-In Theatre was home to a flea market where vendors set up folding tables to sell inexpensive antiques and collectibles—tools, costume jewelry, and vintage kitchenware—as well as old books and magazines, arts and crafts, batik wall-hangings, wrap-around skirts, discounted T-shirts and underwear and Cape Cod sweatshirts in the pale colors of saltwater taffy. I loved looking through the antiques and old books, hoping for one of those rare and wonderful moments when I would find something appealingly quirky that had unexpected relevance to my current circumstances. During a visit to the flea market the previous summer, not long after Malcolm had admitted to me that he couldn't cook a single dish, I'd found a British parody from 1930, *Take Forty Eggs: A Comprehensive Guide to Cookery and Household Management*. I bought the book for Malcolm, who adored its loopy humor, like a recipe for Parrot Pie that began, "Take one parrot or twelve parakeets . . ."

The sun was already strong when I got to the flea market, the heat from the blacktop pulsing through my rubber flip-flops.

I walked by the tables of Red Sox baseball caps and Ray-Ban look-alike sunglasses to the back rows, where antiques vendors had spread their wares on tables and tarps under the vast movie screen. I made my way slowly past old fishing rods, crystal candy dishes, and Fiestaware, to the middle row and a table of costume jewelry, where I sifted through a bowl of earrings in search of something that might work with my costume. When I looked up, I saw Henry in the next row, sorting through a pile of yellow slickers.

"Expecting rain?" I said, walking up to him.

He smiled broadly.

"Fancy meeting you here!"

I had been dying to see Henry since the day before at the swap shop, and it was hard not to lean in and kiss him. But my parents had friends who frequented the flea market, so I kept a reasonable distance and hoped Henry's ruse about meeting me there included a plan to go somewhere together before heading home. We both made an effort to chat somewhat formally, like employer and employee who had run into each other unexpectedly. I asked if Tillie was with him.

"She finds old things depressing."

We wandered, together and not together, from the tool vendor to a display of cheaply framed photographs of bright orange sunsets. Lingering over a table covered with used books, we smiled at each other when a woman in Bermuda shorts strolled by, glanced at a biography of the Roosevelts and sneered to no one in particular, "Eleanor and Franklin *who*?"

Holding up a copy of *The Bluest Eye* by Toni Morrison, I asked Henry if he had loved it as much as I did. When he confessed he hadn't read it, I put down fifty cents and bought it for him. I spotted a tattered paperback of *Winesburg, Ohio*.

"Hey," I said to Henry, "you know Franny's friend Jeremy? Did you ever read his collection of short stories based on these, but set at Choate?"

Henry looked confused, as if he'd forgotten my connection to his son.

"Franny's friend?"

Feeling foolish for mentioning Franny, I hoped that Henry didn't remember my hanging out with him at the party in June, let alone the night of the lobsters. To get him to stop thinking about Franny, I continued talking about Jeremy. "I think Jeremy won some kind of prize for it."

"Yes, that's right," Henry said, sifting through a stack of old *Life* magazines. "He was a precocious one, that's for sure. Those stories weren't half bad. Hasn't he sold a novel? About a forbidden love affair in Nepal?"

"Yes, and it's amazing. Malcolm adored it, gave him a good deal for a debut author. It's fascinating—set in a leprosy colony, if you can believe it. It tells the story of a romance between a young girl who lives there and the doctor's son. It's beautiful."

Henry looked confused and annoyed. I realized my blunder immediately; why would Henry, frustrated by Malcolm's lack of interest in his own work, want to hear about Malcolm's discovery of an exciting young writer—his own son's friend, in fact? How stupid of me to talk about Jeremy and Franny, both closer to my age than to Henry's, which probably reminded Henry I was young enough to be his daughter, or his son's girlfriend. I cursed myself for not having thought of this before babbling about Jeremy.

We walked over to tables of sweatshirts, T-shirts, and socks, but Henry seemed to have lost interest, to have forgotten his ostensible reason for coming to the flea market in the first place. "So no socks?" I said, holding up a pair of white tennis socks.

"I don't need socks."

I sorted through a pile of T-shirts with silly slogans, looking for one that might amuse Henry. I held up one that read GAG ME WITH A SPOON, which Henry had recently declared "an unfortunate and classless expression."

"How about this, then?" I said. "Your favorite."

He looked pained to see the slogan and walked toward a table of discounted windbreakers, which he sorted through as if looking for his size. I caught up with him and asked if he was OK. Looking around to make sure no one was watching, I ran my finger beneath the hem of his shorts.

But without looking at me, he said, "I should get back. I've been gone long enough. We've got people coming for mixed doubles."

32

I was unsettled the rest of the day by Henry's brusque departure from the flea market. When the phone rang late that afternoon and I overheard my mother saying that she'd see if she could find me, I had the hopeful thought it was Henry calling to say he was sorry, though he had never called our house before and didn't really have anything to apologize for.

Perhaps more surprising, it was Jeremy. He cut right to the chase, explaining that he'd gotten my number from Malcolm and that he was calling to ask if he could stay at our house when he came up to the Cape that weekend for the book party. He would be catching a ride with Malcolm, who would be staying with friends in Provincetown.

"It's only two nights," he said. "I assumed I'd being staying at Franny's, but I couldn't reach him in Maine and when I called Henry and Tillie's place just now, Tillie suggested I find some-where else to stay. She said their house is going to be overrun with guests."

I wrapped the phone cord around my finger and then un-wound it.

"That's so kind of you," Jeremy said, in answer to my

silence. "Are you sure you don't want to give it a little more thought?"

"I didn't say no," I said, wishing that I had. Jeremy was so unpredictable, I was worried it would be awkward to be together with him and my parents. "Are you sure you wouldn't prefer to convince Franny to let you stay? I can't imagine they can't find a place for you to sleep." Wasn't he like family to them?

"Like I said, the house is full. Plus, Franny's coming with Lil. How can I say this?" He paused. "She takes up a lot of space. She's been known to air-dry her diaphragm on the windowsill. In the kitchen."

We laughed, and I was reminded of the appealing side of Jeremy's bluntness. He may not be open, but he was honest. I told him I'd check with my parents and get back to him.

I found my mother in the living room scrutinizing the couch, which she had been complaining was uncomfortable since it had arrived at the beginning of the summer. Its purchase had been a rare misstep; she was a good decorator who insisted on balancing comfort and design.

"For the life of me, I can't figure it out," she said, shaking her head. "I know this couch. I've ordered this couch for clients. It was a sure thing. It must be a manufacturing flaw."

I flung myself onto the couch on my stomach, sinking into the soft linen cushions.

"It's not bad like this," I said.

She pushed aside my legs and sat down on one end.

"It's not meant for that. It's meant for conversation."

I turned over and sat up. She was sitting stiffly, like a well-bred Victorian woman trained never to let her spine touch the seat back.

"Relax," I said.

"Watch what happens," she said. She leaned back and sunk

into the cushions, her body slumped down like a rag doll. She flung an arm up and waved it around. "I can't even hold a drink or reach for an appetizer." She pushed herself up. "This was an enormous mistake."

"Speaking of mistakes," I said, sitting up, "a guy I know, a Hodder, Strike author, asked to stay here over Labor Day weekend. He's coming up for Henry and Tillie's book party. Would it be okay if he stayed here, just for two nights?"

"A writer?" my mother said. The offense of the couch forgotten, she looked at me expectantly. I knew where this was going. "What's his name?"

"Jeremy Grand. Né Greenberg."

"Jewish!" She slapped her hands on her thighs. "How interesting. How old is he?"

I shrugged. "Older than I am, younger than thirty. Arrogant beyond his years."

She opened her mouth to speak, but I cut her off.

"No, he's not a romantic interest."

She smiled at me and shook her head. "Oh, Eve—never say never. A bookish girl like you—you could be a wonderful muse to a writer."

The thought of my inspiring Jeremy was almost absurd enough for me to be able to overlook the slight in her words. My mother asked about Jeremy's book, and I told her the truth—that I thought it was original and beautiful. I said it would probably be a big success. She clasped her hands together.

"Ooh, I like him already!"

I called Jeremy back and told him the guest room was his for the weekend.

Sifting through a pile of mail after I hung up the phone, I discovered that I'd received a message from Franny too. A postcard from Maine, and the first I had heard from him since our night together. The card had a photograph of a big, shiny red lobster superimposed over a map of Maine with the words YOU CAN'T BE SAD WHEN YOU HAVE LOBSTER! below. On the back was a short message in blue crayon: *"So Maine is supposed to be the best place for lobster, but we know better! Heading back to the Cape for Labor Day—see you there?"* He had signed not with a *love*, or a *from* or an *xoxo* or even the breezy publishing favorite *all best!* but with a drawing of a lobster pot and the letter *F* written with a looped flourish.

I didn't know what to make of this. Did he know I was working for Henry? Was he giving me a heads-up, relieving his guilt at not being in touch? Or did he want to see me? Worse, would he figure out what was going on between me and his father? I was relieved that he hadn't included a return address because I had no idea how I would have responded.

Dear Franny:
So nice to hear from you! Funny me, I had thought that after our night together, we might have continued our path toward getting to know each other by perhaps exchanging a SINGLE WORD. Like maybe this one: Lil.

Dear Franny:
Sorry I haven't been in touch. Have been totally wrapped up in a new job, the description of which suddenly changed in ways I can't even begin to tell you!

Dear Franny:
Roses are red
Violets are blue,

You're very sexy,
But your father is too.

Dear Franny:
What you may have heard is true. I can't quite explain it
myself.
   Forgive me.

33

After dinner I took the rare step of calling Henry at home. As the phone rang, I prayed that Tillie wouldn't answer. When Henry answered, I said, "Thank God, it's you."

"Now, that's what I call a delightful greeting," he said.

He seemed back to himself, and agreed to slip out in the morning and meet me for a swim at one of my favorite places while Tillie was taking an early morning walk with a friend in Provincetown.

Hidden in the woods of South Truro, at the end of a rutted dirt road that twists through a forest of pitch pine, is a string of freshwater kettle ponds. Slough, Spectacle, Herring, Horse Leech. The ancient ponds are not magnificent like the ocean, but beautiful in their quiet stillness, with water so deep that when you dive down and open your eyes, it looks like nothing at all.

It was just after 8:00 a.m. when we met at Horse Leech, and we had the place to ourselves. We decided to swim across the pond and back. The water was cool. We slid along the surface beside each other, matching stroke for stroke in a way that surprised me as I had assumed that I would be the faster, stronger swimmer. When we reached a grove of lily pads near the other side of the pond, we stopped and treaded water, catching our breath. Henry floated on his back for a while, staring up at the sky. A few minutes passed and, without exchanging a word, we started back. I felt buoyed by relief to be with Henry again, back in our easy and natural rhythm together.

Dappled sunlight warmed the towels we had left on a patch of dry ground close to the water. I stretched out on my back. A bright blue dragonfly landed on the sand beside my fingers and, after a moment, lifted up like a helicopter and flew off. I closed my eyes and said, "I think I have never been so content." Henry didn't answer. When I opened my eyes, he was sitting beside me, tossing sticks into the water.

"I'm aware what a cliché this all is," he said. "Me. You. Mostly me."

My heart sank. Henry rested his elbows on his knees and put his head in his hands, combed his fingers through his hair, which was longer when wet, nearly long enough for a pony tail. I waited for him to continue. He turned toward me and lay on his side. He reached out and put a hand on my stomach.

"Can we not analyze it?" he said, as if I was part of the conversation going on in his head. "Not diminish this interlude by noting the obvious—you get to feel older and recognized, I get to feel young and admired?"

I wasn't sure what to say, how to handle this introduction to his angst. He was half right. I no longer considered him old, and I did admire him. But being with Henry hadn't made me feel older. It had made me feel, for once, my age, myself.

His use of the word *interlude*, while not a surprise, stung. I wished, again, I hadn't brought up Franny and Jeremy, hadn't reminded Henry of his age, and of mine. Or of how happy I was.

I wasn't naïve enough to think that ours would be a long-term affair, but nor was I ready to be pushed away so soon. Looking at his worried face, I knew that to stretch this out a little longer, I had to play the part, to be his fun-loving cliché, and not let on how much I liked being with him, in all ways. I rested my hand on his shoulder and ran it slowly down his arm.

"I've found, these last few weeks, that not thinking too much really is the ticket," I said.

Henry's face relaxed.

"That's my girl," he said, throwing his leg over mine.

part four

September 1987

34

When I got to the house the next morning, I was surprised to find Henry and Tillie sitting in the Adirondack chairs overlooking the tennis court. They had pulled out the little wooden side table in front of the chairs and were sharing it as a footrest, their toes nearly touching. Henry was holding the *Times* magazine and Tillie the Sunday book review. I took a few steps toward them. I didn't want to make my presence known but couldn't bring myself to walk away. Their renewed companionship, so soon after our conversation at the pond, was unsettling. I stepped behind the bushes, close enough to hear them working a crossword puzzle.

"'Cry of jubilation or guilt.' Six letters, second letter *D*, last letter *T*," Henry said.

I heard Tillie say, "*I did it.*"

"Precisely," Henry said. "'Run-scoring bunt' . . . *Squeeze.* 'Verdi slave girl' . . . *Aida.* Ah, here's one for you: 'Vreeland replacement at *Vogue.*' Nine letters."

"Like I read *Vogue!*" Tillie said. "But because I love you: *Mirabella.*"

"You're a wonder," Henry said.

I turned around and walked into the house, saddened and confused by Henry and Tillie's relaxed intimacy, and by the break in their routine. From the kitchen, I could see that the door to Tillie's office was only half closed. With a quick glance back outside, I pushed it open. The desk was a mess, covered with papers and books, clamshells holding paper clips and thumb-tacks, and a piece of driftwood shaped like a gun. But the futon along the wall was open like a bed, taking up much of the room. A plain white sheet and a thin patchwork quilt were twisted in a jumble at the bottom of the mattress. On the floor beside it, I saw Henry's reading glasses, his tennis shirt and boxer briefs, an empty bottle of wine and two empty juice glasses.

I realized then that I had assumed, for no good reason, that Henry had stopped sleeping with Tillie once he had started up with me. Had I been wrong or had Henry, having put me at a more manageable distance yesterday at the pond, only now drifted back to Tillie? It seemed ridiculous to feel betrayed that Henry had slept with his wife, but I couldn't deny it hurt. And the fact that it was here, in Tillie's office, somehow made it worse, suggesting this was not routine married sex, but that they had been too overcome with desire to go upstairs to their bedroom.

On a little table by the futon, beside a glass vase of dried wildflowers, was a small black notebook. I found it hard to be-lieve that Tillie would keep a journal, but the thought that she might, that she took the time to write down her feelings simply and directly, without the subterfuge or embellishment of poetry, that there could be words there to reveal what was really going on with her and Henry, was irresistible. I was about to pick up the notebook when I heard voices outside. I managed to get back to the kitchen before Henry and Tillie walked inside.

I didn't share my unease with Henry. He was in a good mood, standing behind me at my desk, humming as he massaged my shoulders and kissed my head. He offered to drop me at home on his way to Provincetown to buy booze for the party, but I had my bicycle.

Instead of going straight home, I rode to Corn Hill for a swim, hoping to clear my mind. I walked along the beach and stripped down to my underwear and dived in. Swimming toward the jetty, I tried to let the water work its magic. I focused on the gentle pull of the waves, the strands of seaweed tickling my thighs, and the gentle bump of tiny jellyfish as soft as bubbles against my skin. But my thoughts kept going back to Henry and Tillie and the open futon, to the book party and the antique dress I'd found for my costume, and to how much I wanted to look ravishing enough to make Henry think only of me.

35

For the rest of the week, as the party approached, Henry was busier than usual, intermittently working on a proposal for a Talk of the Town on the longest-serving doorman in Manhattan—who happened to work in Henry's building—and doing chores to prepare for the big event. Tillie checked in with Henry several times a day, interruptions that didn't appear to disturb him in the slightest. But it certainly bothered me how the party planning was bringing the two of them together. Perhaps the book party, originally meant to mark their anniversary, was a reminder of their long history and that wherever and however they meandered, they always came back to each other. Maybe that's what marriage was, a Mobius strip of togetherness, so that no matter how much a couple twisted and turned away from each other, even toward someone else, the attachment remained.

Since the pond, and Henry's apparent reconciliation with Tillie the day after, Henry seemed to be dialing down our affair, but subtly, as though following instructions from a manual on how to ensure a soft landing. There was no abrupt break, nothing I could put a finger on, just a drifting away that seemed almost too easy for him and confirmed my belief that he had been down this road before.

He still caressed my shoulder when he walked by, but often absentmindedly, without lingering long enough to see how I might react. I tried not to care, but his diminishing attention hurt. Flashes of our time together popped into my head, but in the way that you can remember something wonderful and doubt whether it had unfolded as you had thought at the time. Our rolling on the sand, our sated dozing, limbs intertwined, in the motel room—had I only convinced myself that Henry's joy was as intense as mine?

I had been so pleased with how well I had stayed in the moment with Henry and resisted thinking about a future with him. But now that he was turning away, I realized how unready I was to let him go.

I decided not to make it easy for Henry to quit me. I continued to play the free spirit, dressing in a way that I hope looked effortlessly sexy, showing up to work in skimpy halter tops and sundresses. I wanted Henry and wanted him to want me back— at least for a few more weeks—and I didn't feel it was something I should hide or apologize for.

36

I didn't usually work on Saturdays, but Henry and Tillie asked me to help set up for the party, so I drove over to their house in the afternoon before meeting Jeremy and Malcolm at Truro Center.

"Excellent, you're on chair duty," Tillie said, as I got out of the car. She pointed me toward Henry, who was standing on the lawn by the front porch with a piece of paper that looked like a map. In front of him were two stacks of tables, one of round table tops and one of rectangular, legs folded beneath them, and several stacks of folded white wooden chairs, all rented for the party. Henry kept looking at the paper and then the chairs and the yard and back at the paper as though it were all a puzzle beyond his ability to solve.

"Spatial relations. Not my forte," he said, holding the map out toward me, as if he had neither use for nor interest in it. I took the paper from him. It was immediately clear where the tables should go—three rectangles in the front of the house, for drinks and food, three round ones on the side of the porch with ten chairs around each, and two more round ones at the back of the house, also with chairs, on the flat grass outside the porch.

Before I started to explain the layout to Henry, Lane pulled into the driveway in her pickup truck.

"Finally!" Tillie said. She walked up to Lane's truck holding a tall pile of folded paper bags. As the bags slipped from Tillie's grasp, Lane grabbed them. Tillie said something that I couldn't hear, and Lane said, "'Whoopsy-daisy'? Did you really just say 'whoopsy-daisy'?" and they both laughed. Annoyed by Lane's ease with Tillie, I turned to Henry and asked what the bags were for.

"Paper-bag candles," he said, looking somewhat surprised that I asked.

"For where?"

"To line the driveway, of course," he said. I must have looked confused as he said, "Ah, right, you've never been to the book party. I forgot. Thought you had."

His comment made me feel as though I was an afterthought—like a piece of furniture so plain and functional that you had to think hard for a moment to remember if you still had it in your house or had already given it away.

The phone rang and Henry turned to go inside. "That's probably Franny. Damn him. We really could have used his brawn today. Mind starting with the chairs?"

"Has Franny decided not to come?" I called out, as Henry opened the screened door to the porch. As curious as I was to meet Lil, I would have been relieved to learn that Franny wasn't coming, after all.

"No, no, he'll be here," Henry said. "Too late to be of much use—some to-do with Lil, it seems—but not too late to enjoy the party."

By the time Henry returned, I had unfolded all the chairs that were to stay on the side of the porch and had carried most of the rest to the back. When I returned to the front for my last load, Tillie and Lane were by Lane's pickup truck filling paper bags with sand.

Henry walked briskly toward me and with a quick glance toward Tillie and Lane, took my hand and pulled me around to the back of the house and down the sloping lawn toward the storage shed beside the tennis court.

"What are you doing?" I asked, annoyed that he'd been inside so long.

"Don't say a word and come with me."

He opened the door and pulled me into the shed. It was dark and damp. He pushed aside some old wooden tennis rackets hanging from the ceiling and sat on the bench along the back wall, a devilish smile on his face.

"Oh, no," I said, shaking my head but feeling a little excited both by the possibility of being with Henry again and that he was willing to risk it while Tillie was home. I found it impossible not to return his smile with one of my own. "Tillie's right outside. And besides . . ."

I wanted to say something about the way he'd been with Tillie the other day—about the unmade futon and their lounging together while doing the crossword puzzle—to make him realize that he couldn't have it both ways. And yet, who was I kidding? There had never been a question of his having to make a choice between Tillie and me. Ours was a summer affair. And it was still summer.

I sighed as Henry lifted my tank top and pressed his lips to my stomach. I ran my fingers through his hair, pulled him to his feet. We went at each other quickly, our manner nearly rough. And yet, even before we were done, I couldn't help feeling that it didn't really matter to Henry that it was me there in the shed with him. I could have been anyone at all.

"You walk out first, to the side of the house," Henry said, his face flushed, zipping his shorts. "I'll go in the kitchen."

From the side of the house, I could see the driveway, already halfway lined with paper bags. Lane's pickup truck was gone, as was Tillie's station wagon.

37

By the time I pulled into the parking lot at Jams, Malcolm and Jeremy were already there, leaning against Malcolm's red Mazda convertible. I stepped out of the car and went to kiss Malcolm on both cheeks, as was his custom, but he stopped me at arm's length and took my hands. "Yowza!" He looked me up and down, nodding at my loose hair, which had grown lighter in the sun, and my bright red tank top and short denim skirt, a summery outfit that was a far cry from the loose black vintage clothes I'd favored in New York. "You are literally sun-kissed," he said. "Or *something* kissed." Malcolm turned to Jeremy, who was grabbing his duffel bag from the back seat. "Is she not a vision?" he said.

"She is a sight," Jeremy said. It wasn't lost on me that Jeremy hadn't agreed with Malcolm. His hair already frizzed from the Cape humidity, Jeremy looked pale, like he hadn't left the city all summer, and harmless. He stepped toward me and tapped my shoulder lightly. "It's good to see you."

"You too," I said, and realized that I meant it. It would be good to have someone to talk to, even if I wouldn't tell him everything. I'd been avoiding Alva, who I knew would not only disapprove of my affair with Henry but would suspect it even if I didn't say a word.

Despite pleading with my mother not to go out of her way to prepare for Jeremy's visit, she had spent the morning going to Hillside Farm for fresh corn and tomatoes, Hatch's in Wellfleet for swordfish steaks, and Provincetown for smoked bluefish dip and a wheel of Camembert. "We'll make him a real Cape dinner," she'd said.

When Jeremy and I entered the house, the coffee table in the living room was covered with the dip, cheese, and crackers and my mother was sitting on the deep couch, her legs tucked under her, ostensibly reading *Lake Wobegon Days*. Her "tells" were obvious: she wore gold hoop earrings and had on the coral lipstick that she usually saved for going out to dinner or to a party. She stood up, slipped on her sandals, and stretched her arm out toward Jeremy. "Welcome, welcome to our little paradise," she said, beaming at him. "I'm Nancy."

Jeremy put down his duffel bag and shook her hand.

"Nice to meet you." He looked around at the room and out the sliding-glass doors to the deck and the hills rolling down to the marsh beyond. It was high tide. The marsh had nearly filled with water and looked like a lake dotted with small islands of bright green grass. "What a beautiful home. Thanks so much for letting me stay."

"Of course!" my mother said, pushing her hair off her face in a way that was oddly coquettish. "Come, come sit down. You must be hungry and thirsty! Eve, get Jeremy a drink. Do you want wine? Or do you prefer beer? Vodka? We have a full bar. My husband—he's fishing with friends in Nantucket and will be back tomorrow—even has whiskey and rye, though I insist that those are *not* summer drinks."

"A beer would be great," Jeremy said. He blinked several times, and then rubbed his left eye.

I wished I hadn't agreed that we would eat in. With my father away until the next day, my mother had free rein to steer the conversation to her interests, which I was sure meant interrogating Jeremy about his creative process and ferreting out enough information to determine if he and I were romantically involved.

I brought a beer to Jeremy, who was standing behind the couch. His nose was twitching like a rabbit. Was he nervous?

"Please, sit," my mother said.

Jeremy settled into the couch, sinking down awkwardly and then squirming to sit back on the edge.

"Smoked bluefish dip?" my mother asked, pointing to the table.

"That's fish?" Jeremy said. He jumped up to his feet, spilling some beer on the carpet. "Shit! I'm sorry." He took a handful of cocktail napkins and started mopping up the beer.

"Oh, it's nothing," my mother said, looking at me in a way that made it clear that it was definitely *not* nothing. She was particular about her carpet. Jeremy put his beer on the table and walked over to his duffel bag, where he rummaged around until he stood up with a pill bottle in his hand. His eyes were red and puffy, his cheeks covered with a splotchy rash. "I'm so sorry. It's the bluefish. I'm allergic. I should have told you."

My mother looked at Jeremy's face, then at the bluefish dip, then back at Jeremy. "Oh my God," she said.

She grabbed the bowl of dip and marched into the kitchen, where she scraped it down the garbage disposal.

"Can I have a glass for water?" Jeremy asked. He walked to the sink and splashed water on his face. I handed him a glass and watched him down the pills. "Benadryl," he said.

I turned to my mother and with my back to Jeremy gestured for her to put away the swordfish filets that were on a platter on the counter, ready for the grill. She looked confused and then put the plate in the refrigerator and closed the door. She waved her hands in the air, like she could disperse the fishiness. I opened the windows and sliding doors and turned on the ceiling fans.

Jeremy stepped out on the deck, closing the door behind him.

"Now what?" my mother said. "Corn for dinner? How could he not have mentioned this? Who goes to Cape Cod and doesn't think to inform his hosts that he can't share space with fish?"

I felt bad for Jeremy, who seemed genuinely flustered.

"Maybe it's a rare occurrence," I said. "It's not the end of the world. Can't we just make some pasta with meat sauce?"

"We can," she said, looking in the refrigerator for the leftover sauce, "providing he's not a vegetarian."

I brought Jeremy his beer and sat on the deck with him. He took a long swig.

"I am so sorry. I should have told you. Sometimes I have a reaction like that and sometimes I don't. It's a little like Russian roulette, but it's been a while since it's happened at all. I thought maybe I had outgrown it."

"You might consider restricting your vacations to the desert," I said, trying to make him feel better.

He looked up at me, his cheeks still splotchy.

"Honestly, I try to forget about it," he said. "My father has the same allergy and he lets it rule his life. Doesn't go to restaurants or shop in stores that sell fish. He can't even relax at the beach. I refuse to live like that. To be like him." He rubbed his eyes. "Do I look awful?"

The red circles around Jeremy's watery eyes made him look like a raccoon who'd recently been crying.

"Not at all," I said, thinking how much I liked this Jeremy, with his defenses down. "Your allergy is quite becoming."

38

The dinner debacle took the edge off my nervousness about hosting Jeremy and the pressure off my mother from performing perfectly for the young writer. We lit a mosquito coil and ate our bowls of pasta outside. Jeremy had a second beer, and then a third. My mother gave herself a second generous pour of wine. By the time we finished our pasta, Jeremy's face was back to normal, but he and my mother were slouching in their chairs. My mother's questions got more personal. Jeremy didn't seem to mind.

"When did you know you were a writer? Did you always know?"

"I wrote like a madman from the age of ten."

I wasn't sure if I believed him.

"Eve dabbles in writing, you know," she whispered, as if she was sharing some shameful secret. She refused to take my writing seriously, although I couldn't completely blame her as I hadn't published anything since college and didn't share my drafts with her.

My mother went on: "But there has to be a fire, not just an

ember, and a true gift to make it a worthy vocation. Eve's older brother, Danny, you know, has a gift. Math is like music for him, and he has perfect pitch. It's extraordinary."

"Mom, Jeremy doesn't want to hear about Danny."

She continued as if she hadn't heard me. "The way I see it, there is a fire or there is not. Danny has that fire. That's all there is to it. And if there is not . . ." She rested her head on her hand, then launched into a story I had heard many times before.

"I was a talented pianist. As a child, I was like a little sponge. I was dutiful and practiced every morning before school and after—for hours every day. I sat straight, held my fingers correctly, played way beyond my years. As a teenager, I poured all the emotions of adolescence into my playing. Or so I thought. When I was sixteen, I auditioned for Juilliard. And was rejected. I overheard the Russian adjudicator say I didn't have 'the touch.' The touch of genius. I was good, I was very, very, very good, but I would never be great."

"Very few are great," Jeremy said, reaching out and patting her hand.

"And if you are not among the very few, what is the point?" my mother continued. "If you are not among the few, then you must be a fan. A clapper. The first to jump up and yell 'Encore.'"

"Do you still play?" Jeremy asked.

"Never," she said.

"Do you miss it?" Jeremy asked.

She looked at Jeremy for what felt like a long time. He raised his eyebrows, like he really wanted to know. She stared back at him, her expression sad in a way I hadn't seen before, and said, "A little."

The disappointment of giving up her dream was clear on

my mother's face. But the story, so familiar to me, now struck me not only as sad, but melodramatic. If she loved piano so much, why had she stopped playing altogether? How could it be enough for her to channel all her creativity into home decorating and all her ambitions into her brilliant son?

39

Drunk and maybe a little embarrassed, after dinner my mother drifted off to her room. Jeremy was far more relaxed than usual, no doubt on account of the Benadryl and the beer. He sat on the kitchen counter, leaning his head on the refrigerator, while I washed the dishes. When I was done, we went outside on the deck, lying side by side on the two chaise longue chairs.

"I like your mother. You're lucky. There was no conversation in my house growing up. Like, literally, none."

"What about your sister? Didn't you guys talk?"

He stretched his arms above his head.

"Debbie? We did as kids. But she got really angsty when she turned twelve. More than angsty. Seriously troubled. She started pulling out her eyelashes and eyebrows, literally yanking them out hair by hair."

"That's awful," I said.

"Yeah, it was disturbing. And no one talked about it. We always had the television on at dinner. *CBS Evening News* with Walter Cronkite. It was either that or listen to my father's humming and the click of my mother's jaw when she chewed."

"Sounds bleak."

"You have no idea. I begged them to send me to boarding school. I heard about Choate from an English teacher and became fixated on it. When they said I could go, I was elated. I thought it would be paradise."

"And it wasn't?" I imagined Choate as a place for golden-haired trust fund kids, not for someone like Jeremy.

"No, it was. I loved it. Going to Choate was like traveling from black-and-white to color. I loved everything—even the din in the dining hall. I could talk there and barely be heard. I learned I could raise my voice, yell even, and it was totally acceptable. Verbal sparring was the norm. And it was OK to be intellectually showy. There was even a lacrosse player—a lanky guy with long blond hair—who would recite French poetry. At my old school, he would have been massacred."

"Did you meet Franny right away?"

"I saw him during my second week," Jeremy said. "He was standing on a chair in the dining hall, singing some sea shanty at the top of his lungs. It was tempting to scoff at his pretty-boy looks, but he was so oblivious to his appeal that it was pointless. I started hanging out in his orbit. For some reason, he liked me."

"What was he like?"

Despite everything, I was still curious about Franny. Maybe I always would be.

"He was unlike anyone I had ever met. He didn't want to argue with anyone. He just wanted to have fun. I had no idea what he saw in me. We were opposites. He was the golden boy, and I was the moody Jew. Once we started hanging out, I could forget how weird it was for a kid like me to be at Choate, where every other kid summered on Nantucket and had grown up hearing about the glory days of Choate's crew team from his grandfather."

I wasn't surprised that Jeremy and I were both drawn to Franny for the same reason—how he made us feel lighter and freer, not like who we were but who we wanted to be.

"Franny loved that I was a writer, but I think he loved the idea of it more than my writing itself. I'm not sure he read anything I wrote. He doesn't particularly like books."

"I know. He told me that. I didn't believe him."

"He liked showing me off to Tillie and Henry, though. I think he knew they would be pleased that he had a bookish friend."

"And were they?"

"They were. And it was mutual. The first time I went home with Franny, for fall break, I sort of fell in love with them."

"Sounds romantic," I said.

"It was romantic," he said. "Not sexually romantic, but, well, you know. . . ."

"I do. What *is* it about them?"

"They're a very seductive family," Jeremy said, rolling onto his side.

"No shit," I said.

"Franny was always itching to get back to Choate, but I always found it painful to leave. Henry was so funny and expansive and knew so much about everything. Tillie was more distant with me, sometimes even cold, but now and then she would talk to me about words, what she called 'the flavor of them.' Being there was like landing on a different planet. It opened up possibilities for me I had never considered."

I was jealous that Tillie had encouraged him.

"Henry and Tillie pushed me to consider writing as a real calling. To take myself seriously and work at it like they did. Meeting them was a kind of revelation."

A revelation. It was how Tillie had described her discovery of Truro in her columns. How I had felt at Henry and Tillie's party back in June. As though a door had opened, revealing a world and a way of being I hadn't believed was a possibility for me.

We lay still, looking at the stars and not speaking.

Slowly, I stood up and stretched my arms toward the haze of the Milky Way.

Jeremy looked up at me, his smile drowsy and sweet. I was tempted to lie back down beside him. Run my fingers along his cheek. But his honesty was unsettling, even a little frightening.

"I'm going to turn in," I said. "Big night tomorrow."

40

The next morning, I found my mother at the kitchen table, fingers wrapped around a mug of coffee, paying rapt attention to Jeremy, who was describing the plot of his novel.

"So it's a tale of unrequited love?" she said.

"I wouldn't call it that," Jeremy said. "More like love unconsummated. Thwarted."

"Well, I cannot wait to read it," my mother said. "And to think, you're not even thirty!"

I poured myself a cup of coffee and sat down at the end of the table.

"He's a veritable wunderkind," I said. "Is that the word?"

"It is, and I'm not," Jeremy said, looking a little embarrassed.

My mother set down her coffee cup and placed her hands, palms down, on the table. She looked at Jeremy sternly. "Do not shy from your gifts," she said. "You are a very lucky young man to have been born an artist. Embrace it."

After breakfast, Jeremy and I set off on a walk down to the marsh and to Corn Hill for a swim, after which I'd promised to drive him to Henry and Tillie's so he could hang out with

Franny and help with last-minute party preparations. It was one of those early fall days, when all the colors seemed dialed up a notch, the grass a brighter green, the water a deeper blue. The sun was warm, but the air cool, as if September were announcing itself.

As we descended the rough path through the beach plum bushes and down the hill to the marsh, Jeremy asked, "Does your mother really think artists are born and not made?"

"That she does. Mathematicians too." I yanked a long thread of honey-colored grass from the dirt and poked it between my teeth.

"It's a rather restrictive view," Jeremy said. "If you need anything to make it as a writer, it's stamina, not genius. No wonder you have trouble finishing stories. It's not magic, you know."

"Isn't it, though? My best stories have sort of . . . poured out of me."

We walked on the edge of the marsh, our feet sinking into the damp dirt as little green-brown crabs scuttled sideways into their holes. A great blue heron glided down in front of us and disappeared into the tall grass.

"Your best stories?" Jeremy said. "And how many would that be?"

"Well, not many," I said, suddenly feeling foolish. "Four?"

"Out of how many?"

"How many stories have I started? Not quite hundreds, but . . ."

We climbed up and crossed the path of the old railroad tracks, overgrown with wildflowers, and then walked down the other side and through the marsh toward the beach by the mouth of the harbor.

"No, how many stories have you finished?" Jeremy said.

When I didn't answer, he said, "I'm guessing you've finished four—the ones that came easily."

"Something like that," I said.

"I rest my case. You need to stop the magical thinking. You have to push through, especially when it's not easy."

The ground was muddy as we crossed the marshy inlet between the tracks and the beach.

"Walk quickly and you'll sink less," I said, picking up my pace.

"Like run fast when it's raining and you'll stay dry?"

I laughed, happy to have the conversation move off the topic of writing.

We climbed through the bright green dune grass and over the hill and onto the beach. There was a light breeze off the bay. I stripped down to my bathing suit and ran in. Treading water, I watched Jeremy walk in slowly, holding his arms up when the water reached his waist.

"Slower is harder," I said. "It's not even cold!"

"You're kidding, right?"

When the water was up to his chest, Jeremy dunked his head and swam underwater for a while, surprising me by surfacing much farther out. Wet and flattened, his hair nearly touched his shoulders. I swam toward him and then asked something that had been on my mind since the night before.

"Did your escape to Choate help your relationship with your parents at all?"

"It eased the tension, I guess. Made me less angry at them."

"And what about your sister? Did she feel abandoned?"

"She did," he said. "Terribly so."

"Were your parents able to help her?"

"In a sense, yes. They got her to a doctor, and he helped. But it was an affront to them. Imagine, they nearly starved during the war, got painfully thin and lost most of their hair, and then they find themselves in a cushy suburb in America with a beautiful daughter who is mutilating herself so badly that she has no eyelashes or eyebrows. It was hard for them to understand."

I thought of Danny, and how even parents who seem fully equipped to help a child can be at a loss. We swam to shallower water where we could stand.

"Do your parents ever talk about what happened to them during the war?"

Jeremy shook his head.

"You know those Holocaust survivors who seem to have turned suffering into immeasurable kindness? The ones that go speak to children at synagogues to show them the living embodiment of resilience and how love triumphs after all?"

"I do," I said. "Those people are incredible."

"Yeah, well, those people are not my parents."

We walked out of the water and sat on the hot, dry sand. "And you're not curious about what happened to them during the war? And before?" I scooped some sand and started digging a hole between us.

"Honestly? I'm not. I'd rather invent stories. Create people."

Jeremy started digging a hole right next to mine.

"Like Sarita, in your novel?" I reached the moist sand and dug a little farther until my arm was in the sand up to my elbow.

"Yes, like Sarita. I'm glad you remember her name."

"It's easy to remember the name of someone you like."

I pulled my arm out and watched Jeremy dig until he was scooping out wet sand and couldn't dig any farther. We filled the holes in and then set out down the beach to the parking lot. We walked in silence to the dirt road back to Toms Hill and my house. At the top of the road, I stopped to look back toward the bay and the view of Long Point at the tip of Provincetown.

Jeremy stopped beside me. The wind had already dried his hair and was lifting his curls. He looked at me and cocked his head as if to ask what I was thinking. And so I told him.

"You know, you're not such an asshole."

"Yeah." He smiled. "I know."

41

From my vantage point at the edge of the driveway, the kaleidoscope of costumes, bursts of color from feather plumes and scarves, wigs and hats of all kinds, sweeping capes and furry boas, made the crowd on Henry and Tillie's lawn look like a single organism, breathing and preening on the grass. It was a frightening sight, this crowd creature, as if it were about to open its mouth and swallow me whole.

I didn't recognize anyone until I saw a familiar-looking woman in a short calico dress and two long braids wired to stick straight out from her head. It was Alva, appearing as Pippi Longstocking, a playful choice that did not surprise me, as I'd often heard Alva rail against the assumption that librarians were stuffy. When she looked my way, I lifted my hands to applaud her outfit. She smiled and raised her glass, making it clear that she thought my costume was a success. Against the rules of the party, I had revealed my costume to Alva, although I had done so by telephone, fearing that an in-person meeting might lead her to suspect my affair with Henry. She had given me some good ideas for making my outfit look authentic although she had refused to divulge her own costume.

Surveying the crowd, I saw flashes of a Dracula, a Musketeer, a man smoking a corn-cob pipe, and a woman who looked as if she belonged in a Renoir painting; then my eyes rested on a tall, strikingly handsome man with slicked-back blond hair wearing a white three-piece suit and gold tie. As he sipped from a champagne flute, a dead-ringer Holly Golightly, in a sleeveless black dress, long black gloves, and a triple strand of white pearls, tucked her head into the crook of his neck. This swanlike beauty, I was surprised to see, was Lane, who, despite her cynicism about the costume party, had gone to considerable lengths to ensure that she looked stunning. And the Jay Gatsby fellow had to be her father. I watched them whisper to each other as another tall man, also dressed in an elegant white suit and gold tie, approached the pair. It took me a moment to realize it was Malcolm. The three of them laughed and clinked glasses, and as Lane walked away, the two Gatsbys stood closer together, their champagne flutes nearly touching. Malcolm threw back his head in laughter and touched his hand lightly on Eric Baxter's wrist.

A man in a purple brocade cape glided by and wished me "good tidings" as he moved toward the drinks table. It was Dickie Compton. Tillie hadn't been exaggerating when she'd told me about his sewing skills. I started to follow him to get a better look at his costume when Franny came skipping toward me with a broad smile on his ruddy face and his hair hanging loose around his shoulders. He wore knickers, kneesocks, and a brown cardigan sweater. He looked childlike, adorable and happy. In his hands was a worn old teddy bear, which served as a good hint to his costume and gave me something to say.

"Christopher Robin, what a pleasure." Despite the way he had angered and disappointed me, I couldn't help feeling happy to see him. Franny bowed with a flourish, and then stood up, clicked his heels together, and held out his teddy bear.

"Don't forget Winnie," he said.

I shook the bear's paw.

"Charmed."

"He was my best pal when I was little," Franny said, giving the bear an affectionate squeeze. "I rescued him from the top shelf of my closet."

The mention of his closet made me think of his room, which made me think of his bed, our night together, and the last time I had been in that room, when I had rifled through Franny's belongings in an attempt to learn more about him. It felt like a long time ago. Franny smiled at me as if there was nothing complicated between us, no history that might have left me feeling forlorn or forgotten. He greeted me the way you might come upon a book, flip through the pages casually, and recall how much you'd enjoyed reading it. So there it was: I was a fond memory.

"I have no idea who you are supposed to be, but you look pretty," he said, as if he were stating a simple fact.

Disconcerted by how good it felt to be under his friendly gaze, I looked around the lawn. Henry was standing near the house, surveying the crowd. He wore a dapper 1940s-looking suit with a bowler hat. Dressed so formally, he seemed middle-aged. When he noticed me watching, he held up his hand and waved, and I saw that he was holding a big metal tape measure. I was pleased to realize that he had taken my suggestion, after all, and dressed as the city slicker with the country dream house, Mr. Blandings. Too bad he didn't know that Alva would guess immediately. Henry squinted at me, no doubt trying to discern who I was dressed as. Uncomfortable to have him see me with Franny, I was relieved when a woman dressed in a nurse's uniform, Nurse Ratched, I assumed, approached him and started a conversation.

I turned back to Franny and asked about Maine, and Lil.

"Have you met her?" he asked, as if he really was not aware that he had neglected to tell me about her existence.

"I was hoping you would introduce us."

My voice sounded brittle. Franny shrugged his shoulders and sighed. I supposed it was the semblance of an apology. He looked around the crowd and said, "She's dressed as the *Woman in White*. You know, by Wilkie Collins?" He said it as if he wasn't sure about the book himself. I had a feeling that neither of them knew that Lil had picked a character who, caught up in a young man's ruse, had been locked in an insane asylum. "She found a copy in Henry's office and liked the title. And what do you know, she found the perfect dress at the thrift shop in Wellfleet this morning."

So Lil and Franny at least had this much in common: they didn't overthink things.

"There she is," Franny said. "Come with me."

I followed him toward the side of the yard, where I saw a young woman, as frail and tiny as a bird, sitting on a picnic table talking to Jeremy. Lil was such a wisp of a thing, it was hard to believe that she had haunted me for so long. She wasn't tall or blond or bold-looking. She did have long hair, but it was straight and dark and hung down her back like a sheet of rain. She had dark eyes and a long, thin Modigliani nose. Her frilly white dress had a high collar, long sleeves, and folds and folds of fabric that spilled onto the bench beneath her and made her look as child-like and innocent as Franny in his A. A. Milne get-up. Looking at Lil and then Franny in his knickers, it was hard to believe that the two of them, the idea of them as a pair, had tortured me so. They seemed insignificant, even slightly ridiculous. And then with Jeremy beside them, dressed in a plain white shirt and khakis, like a Mormon missionary, I felt caught in a dream where people who couldn't possibly be in the same room, like Marie Antoinette and Ginger from *Gilligan's Island*, were in someone's basement playing Twister.

Lil smiled, showing a perfect set of little teeth.

"Look who I found! It's Goodbye Columbus!" she said.

"No," Jeremy said slowly, as if he were talking to a child. "It's Neil Klugman, the protagonist of the novel *Goodbye, Columbus*." Franny and Lil looked at Jeremy and then looked at each other and laughed.

"The once-and-always know-it-all," Franny said. He gave Jeremy a playful jab in the arm.

"Neil Klugman. I should have guessed it," I said.

Franny introduced me and Lil, who gave me a quick hello. She pinched Franny's cheeks and kissed him on the lips.

"Doesn't Franny make an adorable Winnie the Pooh?" she said.

Jeremy looked at me, confused.

"Christopher Robin," I whispered to Jeremy.

"Got it."

Lil reached out both hands to Franny.

"Come," she said, giggling. "We must find you some honey!"

I watched them walk away.

"Are they high?" I said.

Jeremy shook his head.

"They're always like that."

"Good costume," I said, nodding at his outfit.

Jeremy shrugged. "I hate dressing up and this was easy," he said. "I mean—I'm not trying to draw parallels between myself and Roth."

I couldn't help smiling.

"Are you aware of your tendency to emphatically deny your innermost thoughts, thereby revealing them?"

"Do I do that?" he asked. He looked at my long dress and the bows in my hair. "And who are you dressed as? Laura Ingalls grown up and gone to a fancy party?"

"Cute," I said. "But slightly more obscure. Think British."

I was about to give him another clue when I felt a hand on my lower back and whipped around to see Henry walking by, whistling with exaggerated nonchalance and heading for the drinks table. When he got there, he turned and winked at me. I was a bit annoyed at his indiscretion, and at how his attention gave me a rush. I was relieved he hadn't approached me while I was talking to Franny. I wasn't ready to be around both of them at once.

Before I could ask Jeremy to get me a drink, a woman in a honey-colored gown with voluminous skirts and a bodice so low-cut her nipples threatened to make a cameo twirled beside Jeremy and curtsied slowly, managing not to spill champagne from her glass. I looked at her blond wig, dark lips, and the wide pearl choker around her long neck and was astonished to realize that it was Tillie. She was always striking, but she had utterly transformed herself. Presumably playing the part of whoever she was—Caroline Bingley? The Marquise de Merteuil?—she stretched her arm toward Jeremy and watched him with an eyebrow raised until he took her hand and kissed it. Only then did she acknowledge me with a nod and an obvious once-over, from the ringlets in my hair and my pink cheeks to the length of my frilly dress and the bows on my shoes.

"Now here's a perfectly appropriate couple," she said. "Allow me to extend my warmest congratulations on your union. Mazel Tov!"

Jeremy watched her twirl her way to the side porch.

"What was that about?" I asked.

"Isn't it obvious?" Jeremy said.

I thought about some of Tillie's remarks to me, including this latest, and suddenly saw it clearly.

"Is Tillie a little bit anti-Semitic?" I asked.

Jeremy gave me a knowing look.

"Isn't everyone?"

42

The party was not unfolding as I'd hoped. Franny was completely unbothered by my presence, acting as if he barely remembered me. Together with Lil, he was spritely and free to the point of annoyance. Tillie continued to treat me coldly. And Henry was confusing me with his on-again, off-again flirtation. I even felt slightly betrayed by Malcolm, who had never mentioned that he knew Lane's father, which I suspected played a part in his eagerness to come to the party. I wouldn't have been surprised if he hadn't brought the latest edits of Henry's manuscript as promised.

I asked Jeremy to get me something strong to drink. Watching him weave his way through the crowd, the drabness of his costume came as a relief. He hadn't overreached with an impressive and obscure outfit, but had hewed close to his comfort zone, fulfilling the task at hand and leaving it at that.

What had seemed so pretentious back in New York—his disavowal of his suburban Jewish background and determination to overcome it, his attraction to Franny's world in hopes of siphoning off some of Henry and Tillie's creativity—had reminded me, unflatteringly, of myself. I didn't like to acknowledge how we shared both a discomfort with who we were and a need to be part of a different, better place. But now that he had opened up about his family and his youthful angst, I was more forgiving. Jeremy could be prickly and arrogant, but he was honest. He was betraying no one, in his life or in his fiction. His imagination was all that much more powerful for catapulting him away from his repressed upbringing and creating the incredible world of his novel. Thinking of it now, I was puzzled that I'd discounted the man who had written a story that had made me cry.

Jeremy handed me a drink, and without asking what it was, I drank down the whole glass. Jeremy asked if I'd eaten anything. I shook my head.

"Well, then, have at it," he said. "Better late than never." He bent his head forward and leaned in toward me, his hair nearly brushing my face. It took me a moment to understand what he was doing. It was the trick he had shown me at the progressive party, to take a sniff of hair while drinking on an empty stomach. That night, and the idea I'd had of Jeremy at the time, felt long ago. How quickly I'd judged him. I set down my glass and took his head in both hands. With my fingers resting on his thick curls, I smelled the warmth of his hair. Jeremy looked up, his face inches from mine. Before he could say or do anything, I took him by the hand and led him into the middle of the crowd dancing on the back porch.

I pulled the clips and ribbons from my hair and tossed them into a corner. Lacing my fingers in Jeremy's, I lifted our arms up in the air. I moved my hips closer to his body. The music was loud; there was no conversation. Our brows got sweaty, our faces flushed. The crowd around us became a blur, the people and their costumes irrelevant.

When the music slowed, Jeremy pulled me toward him. My head on his chest, I closed my eyes, breathless from the dancing and dizzy from the drink. I let myself relax in his arms as we moved in small circles around the porch. After a few minutes, I looked up at Jeremy, expecting to meet his eyes. But he was looking at something across the porch. I followed his gaze.

Tillie and Lane made an odd tableau, swaying their bodies to the music, their eyes locked, Tillie in her eighteenth-century finery and Lane a sleek Holly Golightly. Tillie held up a cloth napkin and Lane clasped the end of it with her long fingers, turning her body beneath it and stepping in and away like in a Greek dance, until Tillie pulled it taut and drew Lane closer to her. They never touched, the napkin keeping them apart, but the raw intimacy of their dance, between them as a pair, was palpable. Others were watching them too, slowing their own dances and backing toward the edge of the porch to cede the floor to Tillie and Lane.

There was no mistaking this declaration. This was not just a light flirtation; this was far more serious. I had never seen Tillie look at Henry the way she was looking at Lane, and had never seen Lane look so sincere, or so beautiful. They were connected in a way I had never imagined. They were in love.

Henry stood alone by the screen door, watching his wife dance with Lane, and it was obvious that he saw their love too. Henry's arms were limp by his side, the tips of the fingers of one hand holding a small notebook that looked as if it was about to drop to the floor. I assumed this was where he had recorded his guesses of everyone's costumes. Henry's eyes shifted around the porch, not seeming to focus on anything or anyone. At this moment, Henry didn't look middle-aged. He looked old.

Watching Tillie and Lane, it started to sink in that Henry and I had been played for fools. Tillie's coolness to me may have been genuine, but it had also served a purpose. Without the burden of worrying about Tillie's feelings, I had been free to become the distraction that Henry wanted and, more important, that

Tillie needed him to have so she could tend to what had been brewing with Lane. Poor Henry. He had thought that he was the tortured one, that the only ambivalence to resolve was his own. What he'd probably thought had been a reconciliation with Tillie that morning I'd found them amicably doing the crossword, a coming together, or at least a coming to terms, after another meaningless summer dalliance, had perhaps for Tillie been a fond farewell. A last burst of companionship, or love, before making her break.

Henry must have sensed people looking at him. He flipped through the pages of his notebook as though he was searching for something in particular. He looked up and right at me, but without recognition or tenderness. At that moment, I understood how deeply Henry loved his wife and how lost he would be without her. All along, the stakes of what we were doing had been so much higher than I imagined.

"I need some air," I said. I walked out of the porch and across the back lawn to the Adirondack chairs by the tennis courts. Jeremy followed.

"I am such a fool," I said, dropping into one of the chairs.

"You mean about Tillie and Lane? How could you have known?"

He sat beside me. I let him think that the revelation of Tillie and Lane's relationship was the only thing troubling me.

"I never would have guessed either," he said, "but it does explain why Tillie and Henry both seemed so strange this afternoon. I thought it was me, but I guess they've been having a difficult summer."

We sat in silence for a moment, until Jeremy said, "There's something I have to ask you."

Oh God, I thought, *he knows about Henry.*

I took a deep breath and waited.

"Who are you dressed as?"

I had forgotten about my costume, how carefully I had chosen it. I had first considered dressing as Zuleika Dobson as soon as I had finished the book. Henry and I had put our work aside to recite to each other our favorite lines, Henry's in a laughably bad British accent. At first, I was reluctant to dress up as the coquettish Zuleika. It seemed too daunting and presumptuous, a step too far, but after everything that had happened with Henry, my confidence had grown and I had warmed to the idea, not only as an inside joke that would please Henry, but because I wanted to play a femme fatale. It would be the perfect climax to my summer, not only to attend the book party, but to be beautiful and elegant and bewitch the guests as Zuleika would. I told Jeremy about Max Beerbohm and the Edwardian heroine of his satiric novel.

"Zuleika Dobson? That's the first I've ever heard of it. I doubt anyone will guess that one," Jeremy said.

"Henry would have figured it out," I said, and sighed.

"Would he?" he said, sounding a bit wary.

"It's one of his favorite books—he talks about it all the time," I said quickly. "It's not Zuleika he loves; it's Max Beerbohm. He idolizes him: his wit, his satire, his Britishness. Anyone who knows Henry knows that."

I was suddenly overwhelmed with sadness—for Henry as much as for myself. The past few weeks had been so incredible, so liberating. It had made me so happy to make Henry laugh, but also to make him gasp with pleasure. I had known it would end eventually, as sure as I had known the days would get shorter and the nights cooler, but to see it end like this, so unexpectedly, and with Henry so dejected, and so unaware of me, felt hurtful and wrong. Feeling as if I might cry, I told Jeremy I had to find a bathroom.

"I'll be right back."

Inside, the raucousness of the party was jolting, an affront after the scene that had just unfolded on the dance floor. I could barely move in the kitchen, where a bunch of people surrounded a shaggy-haired guy wearing black Ray-Bans and a dark suit, trying to guess what character he was dressed as. "Here's a big hint," the guy said. "I have no name. Here's another one." He bent over the kitchen counter and took a big sniff, miming snorting cocaine. As I pushed my way through the crowd toward the front hall, someone shouted, "I've got it! You're the guy from *Bright Lights, Big City!*"

The bathroom door was locked, so I headed up the stairs, maneuvering around a couple sitting on the steps holding hands and whispering. Their costumes were the most obvious I'd seen all night, but it was still disorienting to witness what appeared to be a romantic tryst between Sherlock Holmes and Hester Prynne of *The Scarlet Letter*. Upstairs, I was dismayed to find the door to the hall bathroom closed and to hear laughter from inside. By now, I not only wanted a moment alone, but needed to find a toilet.

The door to Henry and Tillie's bedroom was closed. I knocked lightly. When no one answered, I walked through the room to the bathroom. I sat on the toilet and rested my head in my hands. How had I missed all the signs of what really had been going on in Tillie and Henry's house? I wanted to find Henry, to say something to him, but what would I say? I looked in the mirror, dismayed to see how disheveled I was. I splashed water on my face and ran my fingers through my hair, which was a mess. My earrings were pinching my lobes, so I unclipped them and left them in a clamshell on the back of the toilet.

From the window, I could see people milling around the lawn and hear the strains of "Rock Lobster." It seemed impossible to me that the party was in full swing, that despite what had happened, what so many people must have witnessed, the festivities continued. I saw Henry, presumably trying to act normal, talking to Malcolm, who had his arms folded against his chest defensively. I hoped he hadn't just told Henry that he still hadn't edited his chapters.

I stepped out of the bathroom and looked around the bedroom. It was just as it had been the first time I'd been there. The white sheets, the casually made bed. Candles everywhere. I remembered how I had thought the bedroom had told me all I needed to know about Tillie and Henry's marriage. Why had I thought that the way things appeared—or even the way people said they were—had any relationship to reality?

On the night table beside the bed was a small silver picture frame. I picked it up. It was a picture of Henry I had never seen before. He looked young and strong, balancing on one leg on a wooden swing that hung from a tree, smiling as though he was in love with whoever was taking the photograph. I would have liked him to look at me that way. When I put the frame down, a small booklet caught my eye. A thin gray journal. The cover read *Nerves: A Novella. Honors Thesis of Henry C. Grey. Yale University, Spring 1955.* I smiled. Henry never told me he'd written fiction. Curious, I opened the booklet.

As I read the first paragraphs, my heart quickened with a sense of déjà vu. The novella began with the description of a girl wandering through a lush garden. Climbing up a wrought-iron fence and peering through its bars toward the sea. The girl, I read, was on the Hawaiian island of Molokai, which was notable for two things: it was shaped like a shark and was home to Kalaupapa, a leper colony.

43

I scanned the pages of Henry's novella in disbelief. There was a lonely protagonist, trapped in the colony. A handsome adolescent boy. I scanned the pages, flipped to the last chapter, to the girl's disappointment, watching from up high in the tree as the boy she loved walked down a long path through the lush jungle. I was so confused. I couldn't figure out how Henry could have known the story in Jeremy's novel—before I realized that was impossible.

I ran downstairs and outside to find Jeremy leaning against one of the Adirondack chairs. When he saw me approaching, he smiled, until I got closer and his expression changed from happy to wary.

"You stole the story!" I said, my heart pounding. I was so outraged and disappointed.

Jeremy blanched. He glanced at the journal in my hand.

Folding his arms and stepping back, he said, "I didn't *steal* anything."

"No?" I flipped through the pages, barely able to speak clearly. "Not the girl with leprosy? The boy she loves? An impossible love affair? From what I've read, it's the same story."

"Calm down," Jeremy said quietly.

A bearded man in a long dark coat and a convincing-looking wooden leg hobbled toward us. "Have you seen Joan?" he asked. "She's dressed like a whale. Can't find her anywhere."

Jeremy shook his head and grabbed my wrist, pulling me farther from the house, halfway down the sloping lawn that led to the tennis court. He turned slightly before stopping. He was on higher ground than I was. His grip on my arm was tight. "My book is nothing like Henry's," he said, towering above me. "I used the scaffolding of it, that's all. It's totally different—not to mention the fact that his writing is completely wooden."

"Wooden? What does that matter?" I said, stepping up the hill to be on even footing with him. "You can't write the same essential story and pass it off as your own."

Jeremy smirked, which made me too angry to follow his convoluted explanation that he'd only taken the "kernel" of an idea, keeping its essence but cultivating it until it was something completely different.

"It's more than a 'kernel,'" I said, my voice rising. "It's plagiarism."

"It is not plagiarism. I ran with his idea and made it better."

"You changed Hawaii to Nepal, as if that makes it all OK," I said. "Are there even leprosy colonies in Nepal? Come to think of it, did you even go there? Or was your trekking adventure a lie too?"

"Yes, I went to Nepal."

Jeremy tried to grab the novella from me. I pulled it back. "Don't!" I cried.

"Artists riff on the same images all the time," he said. "Think of all the still lives in the world. Some are good, and some are hideous, but no one says, 'You stole my idea of painting a bowl of fruit.'"

"That's just dishonest, Jeremy. This is different—you and Henry didn't see the same thing and conjure it differently. You took what was his."

Jeremy shook his head.

"All he had was plot, and plot is fair game. Writers use the same stories all the time and no one cries plagiarism. Look at Shakespeare. He stole almost all of his plots."

"Now you're equating yourself with Shakespeare?"

"I'm not," Jeremy said emphatically. "I'm just saying that Henry came up with a good idea that he executed poorly. I think he's embarrassed by that novella, which I've never even heard him mention. It's probably the reason he went into journalism."

I saw a flash of white in the woods at the edge of the tennis court and heard Franny's low laughter. Jeremy followed my gaze. For a few seconds, we paused in our conversation as we watched Franny and Lil scrambling off together into the woods. Jeremy shook his head like he'd seen this all before. "They can't keep their hands off each other."

I wasn't ready to change the subject. I sank onto the grass, the novella in my lap. Jeremy sat beside me. I asked when he'd discovered it. He told me it was during his freshman year at Vassar, when he met Franny in Truro for Thanksgiving break. Henry had encouraged him to read widely from his library and to borrow anything.

"So you helped yourself to his story?"

"It stayed with me, and so I reimagined it."

Jeremy looked at me as if he was waiting for me to agree with him, to soothe the part of him that, deep down, must have known that what he'd done was wrong. I asked if Henry knew what he had done. Jeremy said, "Not yet, but I'm going to tell him. Maybe tomorrow." His face was solemn. And then I remembered the flea market.

"He already knows what you did," I said quietly.

Jeremy looked confused.

"I told him."

"How could you possibly have told him?"

He looked at the house, as if expecting to see Henry outside the kitchen, having gotten the news from me on my way back outside. I could hear music, the plaintive sounds of a Linda Ronstadt ballad, and the high peal of a woman's laugter.

"I didn't *know* I was telling him. We were at the flea market together in Wellfleet, and I came across a copy of *Winesburg, Ohio*, which reminded me of you and so I told him about your book deal and your novel. I described the entire plot."

Suddenly, Henry's behavior at the flea market made sense. He hadn't been jealous of Jeremy's success or upset about my being so much younger. He had been disturbed to learn that Jeremy had not simply written a novel about "a forbidden love affair in the Himalayas," as he had thought, but had plagiarized his own story. I wasn't sure whether to be relieved or upset that Henry hadn't shared his shock with me. He must have gone home and found the novella, which would explain why it was out in his bedroom. He must have discussed it with Tillie, which was probably why both she and Henry had been cold to Jeremy and hadn't invited him to stay at their house.

I looked up and saw Jeremy staring at me. He looked confused. And angry. In a slow whisper, as if he wanted to delay the inevitable answer to his question, he asked, "Why were you at the flea market with Henry?"

I felt a flush of warmth on my face. I looked down at my lap. I could feel Jeremy watching me, waiting for me to speak. Afraid to meet his eyes, I looked away, which apparently confirmed what Jeremy suspected.

"Jesus, tell me you didn't. First Franny and then his father?"

He stood up, towering over me. "That is seriously twisted. That's like some weird form of incest."

My stomach heaved.

"It is not," I said, trying to keep my voice steady as I stood up to face Jeremy. "And it has nothing to do with your stealing Henry's novel. You're the one who crossed a line here, not me."

"I crossed a line? That's something coming from someone who's been having an affair with a married man twice her age."

"Stop making this about me. You've been lying to everyone since the day you sent your manuscript to Malcolm. If you did nothing wrong, why the secrecy?"

I hated the way he was looking at me.

"Jeremy Grand, Jeremy *Greenberg*—whoever the hell you are, you're full of shit. A phony."

I started to turn away, but Jeremy grabbed my arm and yanked me back. "I'm full of shit?" he said, holding my arm tightly, his voice rising. "I wrote every word of that novel. Unlike you, I actually *write*. Day after day, night after night. All you do is talk about it and whine about how it *doesn't flow*." His voice was so cold. "I work at writing. You just make yourself feel like a writer by fucking one."

I was stunned. My chin trembled. Jeremy dropped my arm and glared at me, waiting for me to say something. I couldn't stand the thought that he'd see me cry. I looked down the hill and, to my horror, saw Franny and Lil, hand in hand, skipping toward us. "Shit."

"What ho, fair friends!" said Franny, stopping in front of us. "What gives? Is this a lover's quarrel?"

44

"Are you guys a couple?" Lil said sweetly. "That's so romantic."

"Oh, there's a romance, but it doesn't involve me," Jeremy said.

"Don't," I said.

"Who's the lucky fellow?" Lil asked me.

Jeremy and I locked eyes, as if we were daring each other to be the first to speak. To stop him from exposing the truth about Henry and me, I tossed the novella to Franny.

"What's this?" he said, catching the booklet.

I explained what it was and what Jeremy had done with it. As I talked, I could sense Jeremy watching me.

Franny seemed surprised that his father had written fiction. "I had no idea," he said, flipping through the pages. He looked up at Jeremy. "But what the hell? You stole his story? You lied to me?"

"Don't listen to Eve," Jeremy said. "It's nothing like mine."

"Which, again, begs the question—why the secrecy?" I said.

"Yeah," Franny said. "Why didn't you tell anyone? Or at least ask Henry if you could adapt his story? You started your novel years ago."

THE LAST BOOK PARTY

"I was going to tell him. And I will," Jeremy said. "C'mon, Franny, you know how I feel about Henry. Of course I'll tell him." I was surprised by his eagerness to convince Franny of his sincerity, as if Franny's opinion of him was more important than anyone else's. "I tried calling him last week. He's hard to reach."

"Seriously?" I said. "You can do better than that. Henry is here every single day."

Jeremy hesitated. "He's been busy this summer . . . with writing and . . . with other things." He looked up at me. I could sense his anger like a physical force, as if my affair with Henry had been a betrayal of him as much as of Tillie. In a tight, menacing voice, he said, "From what I've heard, Henry's been rather busy fucking his assistant."

My heart pounded. I couldn't move. I locked eyes with Jeremy, afraid to look at Franny.

"Henry's having an affair with his assistant?" Lil said. She looked toward the side of the house and the guests dancing on the porch to "Chain of Fools." "Who is she? Is she here? Is it the redhead?"

Franny turned to me and in a quiet voice that hit me like a slap said, "Oh, she's here all right."

"It's not like you still cared," I hissed, but not too quietly for Lil to hear.

"What do you mean 'still cared'?" she asked.

When I didn't answer, she turned toward Franny, who had thrown his head back and was looking up at the sky. Lil collapsed onto her knees. With her dress pooling around her, she pounded her tiny fists against her thighs. She looked at Franny, and at me, and then back at Franny. "Tell me you didn't."

Franny sank to the ground next to her and grabbed her hands in his. She pulled them away.

"It was nothing, Lil-bear," Franny said. "Seriously. It just happened. I didn't mean it. It was . . . a hiccup."

"A hiccup?" I said.

Even if Franny had always intended that I would be a one-night indiscretion, to hear him describe it that way hurt me more than his lack of communication all summer.

Franny glared at me. "Don't kid yourself that you mean anything to my father. It's happened before and it's insignificant. My parents have an understanding. They're solid. Someone like you could never come between them."

Jeremy and I caught each other's eyes. I shook my head, trying to signal to him not to say anything. The night was shocking enough already. But Jeremy was determined to keep the focus off himself. He crouched down on the grass opposite Franny and Lil, who was hugging her body and looking as if she might cry. I picked up the novella, which Franny had dropped on the grass.

"There's been a . . . development," Jeremy said. "Involving Lane."

Franny looked bewildered.

"My father was sleeping with Lane too?"

Jeremy shook his head.

"What is happening?" Lil said, covering her face with her hands.

Franny wrapped his arms around her.

"Nothing is happening. We're good, we're good. I love you."

"Not Henry," Jeremy said. "Lane and Tillie . . . a romance."

"I don't understand," Franny said.

"I think it's serious," I whispered.

Before Jeremy or I could explain, the sound of Henry's booming, drunken voice made us all turn. "Where is he? The lying piece of shit . . ."

Henry stormed across the lawn, his jacket unbuttoned, his tie askew, and his shirt untucked. His face was red. He wasn't dapper anymore; he was drunk. He marched toward us, looking at Jeremy as if all his anger at what he'd seen on the dance floor was now being funneled furiously toward this new target.

Jeremy stood up and with his hands in front of him said, "Hey, hey, let me explain."

I tapped Henry's shoulder, but he ignored me. He pulled his arm back as if he were going to take a swing at Jeremy, but then lurched forward and fell into him. Stepping backward, Jeremy lost his balance and tumbled onto the grass. Henry managed to stay standing.

Behind me, I heard a man say, "Ouch, man down. Any idea who he is?"

"Neil Klugman, I think," a woman answered. "At least that's what I heard someone say."

"Klugman? Is he local?"

I turned around to see them walking away, relieved we were far enough from the house that no one else had witnessed the scene.

Franny got up and tried to pull Henry toward the house.

"I'm fine," Henry said, shaking him off. "Don't trouble about me. I'm absolutely fine."

I touched his shoulder again. This time he turned toward me, but he looked so disdainful and dismissive, as if he didn't know why any of this concerned me, that I realized what a mistake it was to think that I might comfort him.

Henry staggered down the hill toward the tennis court and disappeared into the darkness. Franny ran his fingers through his long hair. He stretched out a hand toward Lil, who barely looked at him but let him pull her up. They walked together back to the side of the house. Jeremy, still on the ground, looked at me with disgust.

I wanted to bury my face in my hands, wipe away the entire night. Instead, I turned and walked quickly into the house. I pushed my way between the guests, through the kitchen, and into the front hall, where Alva grabbed my arm and asked, "What's wrong?" Unable to speak, I shook my head and stepped away. I was almost at the door when I heard Malcolm's West Virginia twang from the living room. "I know who you are, darlin'—I know my Edwardian finery—and my old paperbacks. You, honey pie, are Miss Zuleika Dobson!"

More than a little tipsy, Malcolm was perched on the edge of the living room couch, one arm draped over the shoulder of Eric Baxter, whose shirt was unbuttoned down to his navel, revealing a smooth, tan torso. Without answering Malcolm, I stepped outside and let the screen door slap behind me. Still holding Henry's novella, I walked quickly down the long driveway, not breaking my stride as I hiked up my dress and stomped on one paper bag light after another, snuffing their candles one by one.

45

I didn't start crying until I'd put the car in gear. By the time I turned onto Route 6, my vision was blurred. When I saw the turn-off to Longnook Beach, I made a quick right. Gripping the steering wheel so hard my hands cramped, I took the curves in the road too fast, desperate to get to the beach.

As I expected, the parking lot was empty. I left my shoes in the car and walked to the top of the path that went down to the ocean. The moon was nearly full, shining a tunnel of light on the water and illuminating the sand. But instead of descending, I turned and took the path that climbed higher up the dunes, through the beach grass, despite the KEEP OFF THE DUNES: ERO-SION sign. Bunching the skirt of my dress in my hands, I followed the sandy path up to one ledge and then another, higher and higher, until my calves were burning and my heart pounding. As I neared the top, I pushed harder and ran, until I was at the crest of the towering dune, more than one hundred feet above the ocean. The cool, moist wind whistled and whipped through my hair, lifting it behind me and in front of my face, brushing damp strands across my cheeks and into my mouth. My face was wet and salty, from tears and from the sea air.

With my back to the whole of Truro, I recalled Franny's prophecy when he was pretending to read my palm, that I would find myself atop a tall sand dune at night with a handsome stranger. It seemed like a cruel joke. I screamed into the wind, and then felt stupid for doing so. I wanted to rage at everything and everyone—Henry and Tillie, Franny and Jeremy—and myself. I grabbed my dress by the hem and tried to rip it, cursing in frustration when I couldn't. I bent down and picked up a rock as big as my fist and threw it down the dune, disappointed that I couldn't throw it far enough to make it drop into the sea.

Standing in my long dress above the ocean, bedraggled, angry, and confused, I was at a loss as to how everything could have changed so suddenly, how I could have been so wrong about everyone. Had I been so consumed with Henry that I'd missed everything else? Jeremy was lying to himself—that much I knew. But was he right about me?

I looked at the slanted wall of sand stretching below to the dark beach. It was vast and steep, but I knew the way down. I had done this as a child every summer. I took a step, and a jump, and another, faster and farther, getting more air with every leap, careening down the dune, my feet landing and lifting off the sand and chunks of clay, flying down and finding myself pitching forward and running on the beach, almost falling, until I got close to the water's edge and was able to slow myself down.

Breathless, I walked into the surf, letting the waves splash on my shins and thighs. The water soaked my dress and dragged it down behind me like seaweed. I took the dress off and dropped it onto the sand. I walked up the beach in my slip until the moon disappeared behind a cloud and I felt chilled. I climbed up the dune path. At the top, I turned and looked at the ocean, the waves coming in like shadows.

Without wiping the sand from my feet or my hands, I drove

home barefoot, letting my car drift into the center of the empty road. At home, I showered and then sat on my bed, wrapped in a towel, staring into the darkness. I didn't leave my room when I heard Jeremy come in a few hours later. I slept fitfully. At daylight, I gave up trying. I slipped out of the house before anyone was awake. I didn't spot a soul on the walk down the dirt road to the bay. It was low tide, and I waded through the shallow water and onto the smooth sandbars that stretched toward Great Hollow Beach. The water sparkled a brilliant blue in the sunlight. The lighthouse at Long Point looked close enough to touch. But the beauty of the morning was not soothing or inspiring. It was offensive. Annoying. I walked back to the dry sand and stretched out on my back, closing my eyes against the bright sun.

I tried to clear my mind, but I kept replaying everything: Henry's slumped shoulders as he watched Tillie and Lane. Franny calling our night—me—a "hiccup." The pages of Henry's novella. The moment when I realized Jeremy had been lying the whole time. The sting of what he said about me.

When I got back to the house, my parents were weeding the garden. Jeremy was gone.

part five

September 1988

46

Every morning when I stepped outside, the rush of hot, muggy air still shocked me. This was Florida in late September, and the heat was relentless. My hair was always frizzy, my inner thighs sticky. No matter what I wore, or how high I cranked the air-conditioning in my Chevy Nova, by the time I walked through the parking lot and into the chilled offices of the *Citrus County Chronicle*, I was wilted.

Florida's sameness, its unceasing summer weather and endless flat terrain, seemed like penance, as if living someplace where nothing changed, where it was impossible to remember what season it was, let alone what month, was what I deserved for looking in all the wrong places to change myself.

Nearly a year had passed since I'd started as a reporter at the *Chronicle* in Citrus County—a swampy, rural area that hadn't had a citrus industry since the freeze of 1895 and was now known only for fish camps, manatees, defunct phosphate mines, and a few low-rent retirement communities, including one called Beverly Hills. The western edge of the county was coastal, but there wasn't a legitimate beach to be found; you had to paddle through the mangroves for more than half a mile into the Gulf of Mexico to get to water that was more than waist deep. Inverness, the county seat, was a sleepy town. Its charm, if it could be said to have any, didn't come from the brick courthouse in the small central square or the two blocks of basic mom-and-pop shops ringing it, but from the chain of lakes abutting the town and the Withlacoochee River beyond. Inverness couldn't have been further from Truro in landscape or sensibility, which, for me, made it perfect.

I lived in a two-story town house off US Highway 44 East, about a mile from the office, paying less than a third of my monthly rent in New York. I had a small front porch, large enough to serve as a landing pad for the morning newspaper, a screened back porch, a small kitchen and living room, two full bathrooms, and two bedrooms. The building was new Florida construction, which meant it was moderately attractive but shoddy, with walls thin enough for me to hear the newlyweds next door argue as if they'd been married for years and then have what sounded like pretty satisfying make-up sex, followed by the low murmurs of contented conversation. When I saw them in the parking lot, they seemed happy enough, which was a good reminder that relationships, like most things, can be solid and worthy even if they don't look perfect.

The apartment complex had a pool, which no one used but me. After work, I would swim laps and then float on my back and gaze up at the thick oak branches and the fuzzy strands of Spanish moss that hung down from them. Even with my ears submerged, I could hear the high hum of the cicadas. It was a relief to live someplace where I had no history, connections, or expectations.

I had found the job through Alva. When I'd shared my plan to make a fresh start and work as a reporter, she'd suggested Citrus County, where her sister, Camilla, worked in advertising at the local newspaper. Alva, with whom I'd eventually shared everything about the summer, had been one of the few people supportive of my foray into newspaper reporting. "Everyone values the big leap forward," Alva had told me, "but baby steps can take you just as far."

The job was at once dull and fascinating. From day one, I had immersed myself in covering county commission and school board meetings, local elections and parades. I had written about the onset of "love bug" season, when mating June bugs hover in the air and coat the fronts of cars with their sticky bodies. I had covered the trial of a man convicted of shooting his wife in the back with a sawed-off shotgun. At his sentencing hearing, he'd had only one character witness, his high school shop teacher, who testified that while he didn't remember the man doing anything remarkable, nor could he recall him causing any trouble. Deliberating for fewer than ten minutes, the jury recommended the electric chair. Everything was so new to me that I felt as though I was not only learning how to be a newspaper reporter, but was starting life over. I was beginning to understand how the world worked, and how it was both simpler and more complicated than I had imagined.

I liked having daily deadlines and no time to think too long about words beyond their power to say what needed to be said. I'd become quicker at churning out news stories and could practically write a police brief in my sleep. I knew most of the county sheriff's deputies by name and which of the local gadflies monopolized the microphone at zoning hearings because they didn't have anything better to do with their time. I'd written a few profiles, including one about the region's first female alligator trapper, and had been asked to contribute regularly to the feature pages. I'd written a series of front-page stories about a kindergarten girl who'd contracted HIV through a blood transfusion and was at the center of a battle between panicked parents, school officials, lawyers, and doctors about whether she would be allowed to attend public school. The series elicited a record number of letters to the editor, as well as a phone call from my mother to tell me how impressed she was with my reporting and writing. I was surprised by how much her praise meant to me.

I didn't feel like a local, but nor did I feel like a total stranger. I went out for beers a few times a month with the *Chronicle*'s other reporters, who hadn't given up trying to nose out why I had come from so far away for a low-paying, low-prestige job in Citrus County. Typically, I was more comfortable with Sally, the sixty-something owner of the Floral City Antiques Barn and Book Mart, who had barely looked up from her paperback when I had walked in to inquire about a rocking chair in the window. I'd purchased the rocking chair and had become a regular at the shop, where I found and fell in love with books by Florida writers—*Their Eyes Were Watching God* by Zora Neale Hurston, *Cross Creek* by Marjorie Kinnan Rawlings, and *Tourist Season* by Carl Hiaasen. Soon I started dropping in just to talk to Sally, who had vowed to read every secondhand book she purchased for resale. Her eclectic reading made for interesting conversation. From one week to the next, she might want to talk about Edna Ferber, Fyodor Dostoyevsky, or Sidney Sheldon. What I loved most about Sally was that she found something to love in all of the books, even *Jonathan Livingston Seagull*, which she said was either profoundly stupid or illogically profound.

On Saturdays, I volunteered to read to the blind at a local nursing home, marveling every week how the chatter would cease as my elderly listeners got swept up in the story. With no movie theaters or bookstores in Citrus County, there was little to do in the evenings, which had helped me stop circling my old Selectric typewriter and start writing again. At first I managed only a few minutes a day, but eventually I worked up to an hour and sometimes two or three. I still felt queasy when I sat down, but I didn't let fear stop me. I had finished several short stories, one of which had been accepted for publication in a literary journal in Georgia.

Taped to the wall above my desk were photographs of Truro I'd found at the swap shop before I'd left. My favorite was of a short row of gravestones at the old Methodist cemetery at the end of Bridge Road. Tilted and weathered by more than a century of salty air, each was carved not only with the years of birth and death, but with the precise age of the person who had died, in years, months, and days. *Isaac Rich, 23 years, four months, and two days. Eliza Crane, 42 years, seven months, and six days.* The photograph reminded me that every day counts.

I kept up regular correspondence with Danny, who had finally taken a leave from MIT with my parents' hesitant but resigned blessing. He had started on a new antidepressant, the "wonder drug" Prozac, which seemed to be helping. He had moved in with an old girlfriend in Burlington, Vermont, where he had found a part-time job at a bakery, happily taking the 4:30 a.m. shift, which suited his insomnia, and spending the rest of his day tinkering with his girlfriend's loom and mastering the sitar. I shared my stories with Danny. For a math geek who didn't read much fiction, he had an uncanny way of honing in on what I was really writing about, often before I knew it myself.

In his most recent letter, Danny had surprised me by telling me that he had always envied my ability to fly under the radar in our family, to have the gift of not being noticed. I wrote back and asked why families so often act as if there's only one role each child can play—the smart one, the nerdy one, the pretty one—and that if an older sibling claims a certain territory, the others have to look elsewhere to find their niche. *Why can't we both be the brilliant one?* I wrote. *And why can't we do what we love, even if we* aren't *brilliant?*

Sifting through some boxes of books at Sally's shop one Saturday afternoon, I came across a folder of sheet music of old songs that I knew my mother loved. It wasn't the classical music she had studied long ago, but dreamy songs from the 1930s and '40s I'd heard her sing around the house. "Stormy Weather." "Bewitched." "Autumn Leaves." "All of Me." I bought the folder, hoping there would come a time when it made sense to give it to her, when she might sit down at the piano and play.

47

On the last Thursday in September, I got to the office early, at around 9:00 a.m., filed a story on a school board meeting that had gone late the night before, and left the office by 11:00. I stopped by my apartment to change, get my suitcase, and grab my mail, which I would read on the plane. With the air conditioner in my car on high and Suzanne Vega cassette in the tape deck, I settled in for the ninety-minute drive to the Tampa airport. I was looking forward to getting out of the heat, spending the weekend in New York, and finally retrieving my remaining belongings from my old apartment.

On the plane, I settled into a window seat, slipped off my sandals, and started flipping through my stack of mail. It was the usual junk—catalogues, utility bills, a circular from the Piggly Wiggly supermarket—until I saw a large envelope from the Truro library. Inside was a recent edition of *Publishers Weekly*, with a Post-it note on the cover, on which Alva had scribbled *Thought you'd be interested.*

The magazine was like a relic from a past life. I scanned the bulletins on new book deals and editors moving from one publishing house to another. I read an article about the alarmed

industry reaction to the continued expansion of Barnes &
Noble, which with its purchase of B. Dalton Booksellers the
year before had become the second-largest bookseller in America. I read about a new editor at Hodder, Strike who was causing a stir among the old guard by paying exorbitant sums for
commercial books with questionable literary value. And then I
turned the page to find a full-page black-and-white photograph
of Jeremy, wearing a white T-shirt and black jeans and gazing
with great seriousness out the floor-to-ceiling window of a sparse
industrial-looking loft.

Jeremy's novel, to be released at the end of the month, was
already being acclaimed with the usual clichés—"fresh and original," "bold and beautiful," and a phrase long banned at Hodder,
Strike because of overuse, "a meditation on the transformative
power of love." The interviewer asked how Jeremy had chosen
the topic of leprosy, to which Jeremy had responded that he was
drawn to the idea of being isolated physically as well as emo-
tionally.

The end of the profile quoted Malcolm as saying that Hodder, Strike had great expectations for Jeremy's novel and would
be feting him at a book party at Scribner's Book Store on Fifth
Avenue on September 29. I checked my Filofax to be sure I was
right. The party was that evening.

48

I called Malcolm from a pay phone in the airport.

"How's the *Citrus County Bugle?*" he asked.

"It's the *Chronicle* and it's fine, but I'm in New York."

"They've run you out of town already?"

"I'm afraid I haven't written anything noteworthy enough for anyone to take offense," I said.

"Soon enough, cherub. Just don't stay too long. It will ruin you. The truths of the world are not captured in the who-what-when-where-why of an inverted pyramid." It was not the first time someone at Hodder, Strike had dismissed newspaper writing as superficial.

Before I mentioned Jeremy's book party, Malcolm said he was adding my name to the guest list. He signed off by telling me to "shake the hayseeds out of my hair," reminding me of how provincial New Yorkers can be, as if there's no intelligent life beyond the island of Manhattan.

I took a cab to my old apartment, where my former roommate, Annie, still lived with the assistant publicist who had taken over my share of the lease. I let myself in and took a long shower, savoring the intense Manhattan water pressure and trying to calm my nerves about seeing Jeremy after so long.

With the passage of time, and having read Henry's novella carefully, I realized I may have been too harsh in attacking Jeremy. The structure of his novel was different from Henry's and, more important, his language was both subtler and more pointed. His depiction of Sarita's interior life, her girlish yet deeply mature longing, was worlds away from the clumsy way Henry had tried to convey the same thing. I no longer thought what Jeremy had done was completely wrong. But I was still troubled by his dishonesty.

It was jarring to be back in New York. Walking down Broadway to the bus at Ninety-Sixth Street, I moved too slowly, eliciting annoyed stares from several people who pushed ahead of me. I was the only woman in the city not dressed in black. Before I had gone two blocks, I knew that my floral top and flowy white pants, which felt so pretty in Florida, were the wrong choices for a sophisticated Manhattan publishing party. And my plan to travel by bus and avoid the steamy subway turned out to be a bad one. The crosstown bus took forever to come, and the bus down Fifth Avenue crawled in noisy traffic. By the time I arrived at Scribner's, I could see through the store's two-story windows that the party was already in full swing.

I paused for a moment at the door. Scribner's, a Beaux Arts masterpiece, was too majestic a place to enter in a frazzled rush. With its vaulted ceiling, decorative iron railings, clerestory windows, and grand staircase, Scribner's was more than a bookstore. It was the Tiffany of books, a sparkling monument to literature, a place where buying a book felt like an event. Malcolm, who adored the place, had told me that for decades the store's head manager would call in the bestsellers to *The New York Times* for its list, occasionally naming a new book that hadn't yet sold a single copy but that she was confident deserved to be included. Until the late 1970s, the store refused to sell paperbacks. I hoped that Jeremy knew how significant it was, a real vote of confidence in his future, for Hodder, Strike to choose this venue for his book launch. Clearly, plagiarism wasn't an issue of anyone's concern.

I made my way to the back of the store, where Ron, standing at the bottom of the sweeping staircase in a black jacket over a black polo shirt, looked very much the associate editor. He was talking to Mary, who seemed to be in her element, pert and professional in a little black dress, checking off items on a clipboard.

I waved at Malcolm, who mimed an air kiss and turned his attention back to a young woman, no doubt an assistant publicist, who was straightening a few stacks of Jeremy's books on a nearby table. Beside them was Ron's replacement as editorial assistant, Charlie Rhenquist, looking preppy and confident in a navy blazer with gold buttons. He was talking to a petite woman with a helmet head of teased blond hair who I suspected was the editor *Publishers Weekly* had reported was raising eyebrows by publishing books at Hodder, Strike that made money.

Malcolm stepped up to a podium on the landing of the wide staircase and clinked a pen against his champagne glass. Surveying the crowd with impressive calm and an air of ownership, he raised his glass.

"Please join me in welcoming a remarkable new talent," he said, beaming toward the bottom of the steps, where Jeremy stood, hands in his pants pockets and shoulders hunched, looking more bar-mitzvah boy than up-and-coming novelist. Beside him, Mary nudged him gently. Jeremy thrust back his shoulders. He walked up to the podium, cracked open his book, and smoothed the pages with his hand.

Jeremy read slowly, his voice gradually settling into the rhythm of his prose. He looked up from time to time, the words seeming to give him confidence, to make him stand a little taller. I got lost in the narrative once again. He read my favorite scene, near the end, when the doctor's son stands inches from Sarita and holds up his palm. She lifts her trembling hand and holds it like a mirror to his. They never touch, but their gesture pulses with lust and longing.

I exhaled and, as I did, Jeremy looked up. He hesitated when he saw me, then continued to the end of the chapter. The applause seemed to break whatever spell had calmed him enough to read confidently. His cheeks reddened as he nodded his head and stepped down from the podium.

I knew Jeremy would find me eventually, so I leaned against the tall rolling ladder at the bookshelves marked MEMOIR and drank a glass of wine, watching the crowd. Jeremy made the rounds, shaking hands, smiling politely. Finally, he was standing in front of me. He looked timid, which came as a relief and suggested that his conscience had kicked in since last summer.

"Don't worry," I said. "I'm not here to expose you."

"I'm not worried."

"Congratulations. It's a really good book."

I lifted my glass for a toast. He touched his drink gently to mine and watched me take a sip.

"Thanks," he said. "I know."

"Did you not get the memo that young writers are supposed to be deeply twisted and insecure?" I asked.

"I did, and I am."

I looked around the store.

"Quite a party," I said. "I guess none of the Truro crowd is here?"

He shook his head.

"Not a chance. They don't speak to me. I got a letter from Henry last year that said he wouldn't interfere with my 'so-called literary career' but that he had no interest in further communication."

"That must hurt," I said. "I know how much they meant to you."

"Yeah, well, that's over anyway," Jeremy said. "The house is for sale. Tillie and Lane are back in Rome. Franny is living with Lil in Maine. Planning to stay there. He told me he's finally starting to deal with his parents' self-absorption."

That surprised me.

"And Henry?"

I had seen Henry only once, a week after the book party, when I'd gone to his house to say good-bye before he left for New York. He'd shuffled around his office packing boxes the whole time I was there, seeming embarrassed and determined to keep our conversation from anything personal. He handed me a check for my last wages, which put our relationship on a transactional footing that felt worse than his silence. I hadn't known what to say, so I'd thanked him and said I was sorry. He hadn't asked for what. He wished me luck and kissed me on the cheek before turning back to emptying his desk of papers.

"Henry's still working on his memoir," Jeremy said. "He insisted on revising the sections about his marriage, which is understandable considering everything that happened. From what I hear, it's not going well. Malcolm might pull the plug."

I knew that Henry was struggling. Early last spring, long after I was settled in Florida, I'd gotten a letter on that stationery with the engraved initials I knew so well. He had tried to sound casual, asking if I wanted to tap into my "inner archaeologist" and excavate him from the landslide of notes in which he was buried. I'd been relieved that I wasn't tempted, but sad to think of him as lonely and adrift.

"So what's next for you?" I asked Jeremy.

"Not sure. I was asked to teach a seminar at Sarah Lawrence."

"Not an ethics class, I presume?"

"Ouch," he said, pretending that he'd been stabbed in the chest.

"Sorry," I said, meaning it. "Old habit."

"It's OK. I deserved it."

Tentatively, in a way I found endearing, Jeremy told me he was working on a new novel based on his parents' experiences during the war. He was undertaking massive research, about his ancestors and the displacement camps and his parents' years in Israel before they came to America and settled in New Jersey.

"That's bold," I said. "Really."

"It's completely terrifying."

"Honesty becomes you," I said.

He looked a little embarrassed.

"And you? Are you really working as a newspaper reporter?" he asked.

"A regular Brenda Starr," I said. I braced myself for a snide comment about journalism.

"Is that what you want?" Jeremy asked.

"It's a start. The deadlines are making it impossible for me to not finish."

"Then I'm happy for you."

He looked as though he meant it. I told him I had finished a few short stories, one of which would be published in *The Georgia Review* that winter.

"It's not *The New Yorker*, but . . . ," I said.

"Don't do that. It's a great accomplishment—to finish a story and get it published. It's everything."

"Thanks."

"I'd love to read it."

"I'd like that," I said.

We stood awkwardly for a moment, perhaps each a little wary of this tentative sincerity between us. It was a relief to see Jeremy as complicated, yet worthy. To know that the good feelings I'd had about him the morning of the book party may not have been unfounded. An image flashed in my mind, of Jeremy in the front of a canoe on the Withlacoochee River, shrinking in fear at the sight of an alligator. And another, of Jeremy sitting on my back porch engrossed in a story. My story. I smiled at Jeremy, who smiled back.

Mary came up, gave me a quick hug, and told Jeremy a writer from *The Village Voice* wanted to speak with him. "I'll tell him you'll be right over?"

Jeremy nodded and she walked away.

"Your fans await," I said.

"I'll find you," he said.

Jeremy walked into the crowd. The party was humming. Editors, agents, authors, publicists, and editorial assistants chatted and drank wine and laughed as if there was nothing more exciting or important than the launching of a book. Some of them were going to read Jeremy's novel and love it, others were not going to read a word of it and yet proclaim they loved it, and some would read it while hoping on every page to despise it. They would accept Jeremy's new status as a "writer to behold," but none of them would know about the complicated brew of ambition, talent, fear, shame, dishonesty, and hard work from which it had grown.

On the way to the door, I stopped to look at the window display, where stacks of Jeremy's book were arranged in a tableau that seemed to represent someone's idea of Nepal. There were Buddha statues and bronze bowls, Tibetan carpets and photographs of snowcapped mountains. On an easel was the photograph of Jeremy I'd seen in *Publishers Weekly*, blown up to larger-than-life size.

I looked beyond the display to the tall bookshelves ringing the room, every inch of them filled with books, thick and slim, their spines shimmering in hues of brown and gold, blue and dusty red, black and green. In those books were more stories than could be counted—not just the stories on the pages, but the stories that had spurred someone to find the words and write them down. To bring to life imaginary people that, over time, had become as good as real. Were all those authors geniuses? I didn't think so. As I looked up and around the majestic store at the volumes of books, I was sure that many of them, even many of the brilliant ones, were written simply because someone wanted to tell a story.

I stepped outside and let the heavy door close behind me. The air was warm but compared to the intense Florida heat felt balmy and gentle. It would be good to be in New York for a few days. I would clear out the remaining things from my apartment, figure out what I wanted to give away and what would return with me to Florida. I would wander the streets, dig deep into the stacks of my favorite bookstores in search of hidden treasure. And then I would return to Citrus County and the work of figuring out what I wanted to say and how to say it.

A Letter to the Reader

I have always loved being in book groups. Obviously, I love reading and talking about books, and I am always fascinated to learn what's resonated for other readers. But what's amazed me about visiting book groups to talk about *The Last Book Party* is how often I'm asked a question that leads me to a deeper understanding of my own novel. It's never the first question, which is generally a variation on: Is the affair autobiographical? (Answer: No.) Instead, it's often a question about the books that are named in the novel. *Why did you include so many books? Was that your plan all along? Which ones are most important to the story? Are the books your personal favorites?*

At one early event, a reader asked, "Why did Alva suggest that Eve reread *I Capture the Castle*? What does it mean?" The answer that came to mind—"it just felt right"—felt wrong. While it may sum up the strange alchemy of the subconscious and the intellect that creates a novel, it's a little like "because I said so."

"Well," I mused, thinking out loud, "*I Capture the Castle* is narrated by a seventeen-year-old girl who wants to be a writer. But it's clear from her unique and funny chronicle that she already *is* a writer. Perhaps Alva was giving Eve a hint that the way to become a writer is to trust her own voice."

I never planned to allude to fifty-two books in my first novel, but as I spun this story about writers, editors, and readers (including Alva, the wise librarian), book titles started popping up all over. And rightly so. The characters I created *love* books. They love reading them and talking about them. They love what their favorite books say about the world and what having these particular favorites says about themselves. It would have been illogical not to include books in their conversations and thoughts. So, books aplenty. *But why those?*

Three titles were at the back of my thoughts as I wrote. The first two are among my all-time favorites: *Rebecca* by Daphne du Maurier and *Jane Eyre* by Charlotte Brontë. Both novels tell the story of a young woman who is drawn to an older man and struggles to find a footing in his house, where all is not as it seems. Both examine the complications of jealousy and play with costumes as a plot device—a subterfuge and a way to reveal character. Like in *Rebecca*, my novel climaxes at a costume party that the protagonist thinks will be her moment of triumph, but which becomes an evening of shattering disclosures. And in *Jane Eyre*, Mr. Rochester dresses up as a fortune-teller to find out what Jane really thinks about him. The third novel that was on my mind is quite different: *Goodbye, Columbus* by Philip Roth. Not only is this novella a coming-of-age story that takes place over the course of a single summer, but it is also about a young, Jewish man who, much like Eve Rosen, presses his face up against a world and social class that both entice and confound him. So it was too fitting to resist having Jeremy Grand, a writer at once arrogant and insecure, dress up as Roth's protagonist, Neil Klugman, as well as to have him pretend that he chose the costume because it was easy and not because he fancied himself a young Philip Roth.

Setting the novel in 1987 also dictated which books I could include. Eve and I were both born in 1962, so her early favorites included some of my own: for her childhood, *Caddie Woodlawn* by Carol Ryrie Brink, *A Little Princess* by Frances Hodgson Burnett, and the *Nancy Drew* series by Carolyn Keene, and for her early adolescence, the bodice-ripper *Sweet Savage Love* by Rosemary Rogers and the romantic saga *The Thorn Birds* by Colleen McCullough. It was as important to me to include only real books as it was to make sure that the places my characters went actually existed in Manhattan and Cape Cod in 1987. Even in a fictional story—or perhaps *especially* in fiction—having the books, songs, restaurants, and stores of that time period is an integral part of building a world that feels authentic.

The books mentioned also reveal character. Eve's first hint that Henry Grey may not be a stuffy, old writer comes from his bookshelves. There, along with weighty military histories and a worn copy of *War and Peace*, she finds popular fiction like *Rich Man, Poor Man* by Howard Fast, witty books like *Gentlemen Prefer Blondes* by Anita Loos, and even the beloved children's classic *Amelia Bedelia* by Peggy Parish. To signal Eve's growing sophistication as a reader, I had her love *Housekeeping* by Marilynne Robinson, which was published to much acclaim in 1980, and, later, when she moves to Florida, *Their Eyes Were Watching God* by Zora Neale Hurston. The books we read say much about us, reflecting our intellect, interests, fantasies, and dreams at that moment. (That's why revisiting an old favorite is sometimes disconcerting; we remember we loved the book, but we may have forgotten how much we've changed since first getting lost in its pages.) For characters in a novel, just as for people in life, books can externally signal what their holder internally *is* (or, at very least, *might be*). That's why I can't resist peeking at what people are reading on trains and airplanes.

At the same time, books in a book that is at least *somewhat* about books can be a convenient, organic plot device. So I used books to bring people together. Eve and Henry get to know each other by sharing books. Like most bibliophiles, they know that when you share a beloved book with someone you fancy, you're not just saying "here, you might like this," but "in here, a glimpse of my heart." The books that go back and forth between Henry and Eve are not just great stories, but instruments of seduction. By sharing and discussing books, they not only open up to each other but do so without having to admit to themselves or each other what's really going on. Bonding over books lets them turn up the romantic heat without fear of getting burned.

And there was at least one somewhat whimsical choice in my pages. (Surely the author can get one freebie, no?) On Henry's shelves, I put a copy of *Stones for Ibarra* by Harriet Doerr, which won the National Book Award for First Work of Fiction in 1984. Of course, the book reflects Henry's eclectic reading taste, but it's really there because it was published when the author was seventy-four. A debut author at the age of fifty-six, I wanted to give a nod to another late bloomer and also remind myself that I still have plenty of time to write another novel.

So I might've lied to you earlier. The affair in my novel *was* actually autobiographical. But it wasn't the one you thought. It was the one between me and all the books I've loved.

Acknowledgments

Without the wisdom and guidance of Steve Lewis, writing guru extraordinaire, and the encouragement and friendship of my fellow writing group members John Gredler and Cathy Allman, this novel would not exist. Special thanks to Carla Carlson, for inviting me into the writing group that changed my life, and to Karen Pittelman, for her crystal ball and for helping me find the heart of this novel.

Immense thanks to: Suzy Becker, for careful reads and wise counsel; Sally Higginson, for weekly phone calls about writing and life; Genine Babakian, Sally Hicks, Debbie Korenstein, and Lindy Sinclair for thoughtful edits; Maggie Piper, for tough love exactly when I needed it; Saphira Baker, for helping me set goals; Heather Bushong, Mary Beth Connor, Lucia Fiala, Laurie Goodstein, Lillie Hart, Lisa Donati Mayer, and Meg Woods for steadfast encouragement; Michele Sacks for invaluable insights and for still being there; Matthew Thomas and his class at the 92nd Street Y for helpful advice; Randi Davis at the UN Development Programme for supporting the part-time schedule that allowed me to write; Ed McCann and Richard Kollath of 650: Where Writers Read for helping me go public with my writing; Sally Sass, Laura English, and Andy English for Boston and Truro expertise; and the owners and staff of Patisserie R in New Rochelle, where I wrote the first draft of this novel.

Special thanks to Margaret Anastas, for introducing me to the world's greatest literary agent, Doug Stewart of Sterling Lord Literistic; and to Doug Stewart, for guiding me through every step with intelligence, humor, and integrity.

I am grateful every day for the hard work and talents of the amazing team at Henry Holt and Company, starting with my brilliant and endlessly upbeat editor, Libby Burton, who asked for more in all the right places, and Maggie Richards, for being so smart and fun. Hearty thanks to Steve Rubin, Ben Schrank, Gillian Blake, Kerry Cullen, Richard Pracher, Jason Liebman, Pat Eisemann, Caitlin O'Shaughnessy, Jessica Weiner, Carolyn O'Keefe, and the entire publicity team. Thank you to Amy Einhorn and Conor Mintzer for their early and continued enthusiasm for this book and to Chris Sergio for creating the exquisite paperback cover.

Immense thanks to my mother, Mona Dukess, for teaching me to trust the artistic process, no matter how slowly it unfolds; to my sisters, Linda Dukess and Laura Dukess, for always being willing to listen and brainstorm; and to my super-fan in-laws, Jody DiPerna and Roger Schwed. I am also deeply indebted to my late father, Carleton Dukess, for believing in me and teaching me to choose my words carefully.

Finally, more thanks than I can possibly articulate to my sons, Joe Liesman and Johnny Liesman, who somehow always knew when to give me a pep talk and when to ignore me so I could write, and to my husband, Steve Liesman, for his love and inspiration, for making me laugh at just the right times, and for never failing to have more than a little faith in me. This journey wouldn't be as fun without you.

Recommend

The Last Book Party

for your next book club!

Book Club Guide available at

www.readinggroupgold.com